June Goodfield began her ca
and this expertise informs her
contemporary scientific researc.
first novel, *Courier to Peking,* published to wide acclaim
in 1973, was followed by *From the Face of the Earth* – a series
of biomedical detective stories which was made into a
Channel 4 series. A second series, *The Planned Miracle,* about
the world immunisation programmes was made by the BBC
in the late '80s.

From 1982 until 1998 she was President of International
Health and Biomedicine whose remit was to enhance
public understanding of science. She now holds the title
of Emeritus Robinson Professor at George Mason University,
Fairfax, Virginia.

Rotten at the Core is the first in a trilogy about the EU
and Britain's relationship with Europe. It is the result of
meticulous research combined with a wealth of insider
knowledge. June Goodfield travels widely and lives in East
Sussex.

*For David Sayers
with warmest good wishes
from*

June Goodfield

October 2001

JUNE GOODFIELD

ROTTEN

AT THE

CORE

**HOUSE OF
STRATUS**

This edition published in 2001 by House of Stratus, an imprint of
Stratus Holdings plc, 24c Old Burlington Street, London, W1X 1RL, UK.

www.houseofstratus.com

Typeset, printed and bound by House of Stratus.

A catalogue record for this book is available from the British Library.

ISBN 0-7551-0189-8

This book is affectionately dedicated to my friends in Europe,
With grateful thanks for so many delightful hours.

Alain and Annette

Antoinette and Bruno

Françoise

Guy

And most especially, Martin

CONTENTS

Citoyens et Citoyennes de Strasbourg. Prenez garde.
Je vais parler français.
Quand je regarde mon derrière, je le vois divisé en deux
grandes parties...

*Sir Winston Churchill, addressing the Inaugural Session of the
Parliamentary Assembly of the Council of Europe,
Strasbourg, on 10th August 1949*

That Inaugural Session is regarded as a defining moment in the history of the European Union and Winston Churchill's speech its high point. The story goes that a number of distinguished statesmen had given speeches of unremitting pomposity when finally, Winston Churchill addressed some one hundred thousand people assembled in the Place Kléber. Speaking in his execrable French – mostly grammatically inaccurate, but studded with such gems as 'Shitoyennes de Shrastsbourg' – his address on Europe's past history, now 'behind him', and his vision for the future, was received with thunderous applause that some onlookers swear was heard clean across the Rhine.

Churchill was made an honorary citizen of Strasbourg on the spot, a distinction shared with General de Gaulle. No one else has received this honour.

PREFACE

My generation can never forget the politics of the sixties, when the UK twice applied to join the Common Market and was twice rejected. Some of us were so passionately pro-Europe that we sported t-shirts, with 'Europe or Bust' emblazoned across our bosoms. Young, idealistic, and ignorant of the systems of governance in Germany and France, we never guessed the extent to which political decisions were being taken by a political elite, on the basis of twin convictions – guilt, in the case of one country and manifest destiny in the case of the other.

We finally joined the Common Market but, by now many of us are disillusioned and angry, as the extent of manoeuvring and corruption has become clear. The deep democratic deficit within the institution, combined with the lack of both accountability and officials willing to admit direct responsibility, were bad enough. But the actions of the late President Mitterand, whose bribes pushed Helmut Kohl into adopting the euro – though he never thought to ask his countrymen if they wanted it – has been the final straw. Such machinations amount to a cynical betrayal of those who died in World Wars I and II, and whose fate provided – it is claimed – the *raison d'être* for the establishment of the European Union.

The sense of betrayal is heightened by two specious arguments regularly directed by the present UK government against those who disagree with any aspect of Britain's relationship with the EU: first, you are either xenophobic, or advocate total withdrawal – charges that, personally, I resent very much; secondly, the media is equally at fault for their selective reporting. Such knee-jerk reactions reflect both a poverty of policy and a reluctance to engage in open discussion.

The problem is rather one of democracy and consent – an issue brilliantly analysed in Dr Larry Siedentop's recent book, *Democracy in Europe*, that appeared as this one went to press. The crucial question is what actions are governments and Eurocrats willing – indeed able – to take so as to do justice to the sacrifices of the dead? After forty years of closed decision-making, taken by an unelected, un-accountable, self-perpetuating bureaucracy, can the institutions in Brussels ever be reformed? Commissioner Kinnock will try his best, but the odds on success have to be minimal and will decrease as the Community expands. Many believe that only a radical make-over can restore confidence: acknowledging the courage of critics or whistle-blowers, and the strength of their case would be a start. Yet Paul van Buitenen never regained his old job and still remains suspect.

Such issues lie at the very heart of this book. More immediately, the events behind the resignation of Jacques Santer and his Commissioners, provide the back-ground for action that takes place in the limbo period before Romano Prodi assumed the Presidency of the Commission. The scientific data on which part of the denouement depends is, with certain amendments, that available in the summer of 1999.

I have inevitably taken some liberties with people and timing – mostly with DG VI, the Agriculture Directorate. I apologise to Commissioner Franz Fischler for returning him to Vienna. But I have chosen the title of this book with great care. Rotten *at* the Core is not the same as Rotten *to* the

Core. Since not every official deserves our strictures, it was only fair to remove him from the scene. Let us assume that the Sisyphean task of reforming the Common Agriculture Policy finally taxed him beyond endurance.

Other, equally well-known personalities appear in cameo roles. But since this is a work of fiction, the usual caveats apply, even given that some of the events my characters discuss really did take place.

I owe a great debt to many people: first and foremost to many friends in Brussels, especially some ten members of the European Commission staff, and one high-ranking official in UCLAF, the old Anti-Fraud Squad. Others include a most distinguished journalist – for the record, this is neither Colin Blane nor Angus Roxborough of the BBC – three consultants to the European Commission, two of whom are resident in Brussels; various politicians in the UK, some still active, some not so. Without their help I could not have written this book. However, those who recall the unhappy fate of EU whistle-blowers, will understand their wish to remain anonymous. They know who they are: they will recognise their opinions placed in the mouths of characters they may also recognise. I am most grateful to them all.

I must thank many other people also: especially Claire MacLaughlin, a most perceptive and brilliant editor, who worked with me for a year on the manuscript and whose suggestions transformed it; Nick Webb, whose friendship and advice has been available to me for years; my European friends in the dedication with whom I have an enduring friendship and with whom I debated these issues many times – our agreements vastly outweighed our disagreements; Dean Rita Carty and Dr Lorraine Rudowski of the College of Nursing & Health Sciences at George Mason University, who drew on their vast experience to brief me on signs and symptoms at times of medical crisis.

I would also like to thank Dr Andrew Walls of the University of Southampton and Jeff Prather, of the Bailiwick Inn, Fairfax, Virginia, who both separately, shared professional secrets that proved crucial for the plot. I had many serious and valuable discussions about the European Union, with Dr Paul Seabright of Churchill College, Cambridge and was enchanted to learn that he was an advisor to Larry Siedentop, also.

Finally, I am especially grateful to: Angela Skinner, who read the manuscript over and over, and always provided a judicious mixture of helpful criticism and cheerful optimism; Cheryl Lutring, my secretary, who worked untiringly on its preparation for months; the Lutzeyer family whose hospitality at the Grootbos Nature Reserve in Cape Province, South Africa, provided ideal conditions for completing the work.

I am really pleased to be published by one of the newest publishing houses in the UK – the House of Stratus. I am grateful to its Chairman and Founder, David Lane, for having faith in this manuscript and also for attracting wonderful young people to his core staff, such as my editor, Kate Firth. The whole experience has been a joy. The only disappointment was to find that I was not, as I expected, the oldest author in the House. At seventy-three I am a mere babe: one of their authors is ninety-two!

June Goodfield

CHAPTER ONE

The Betrayal of the Ghosts

Violets from Plug Street Wood
Sweet, I send you oversea.
(It is strange they should be blue,
Blue, when his soaked blood was red,
For they grew around his head;
It is strange they should be blue.)

Violets from Plug Street Wood -
Think what they have meant to me -
Life and Hope and Love and You
(And you did not see them grow
Where his mangled body lay,
Hiding horror from the day;
Sweetest, it was better so.)

Roland A Leighton to Vera Brittain: *Villanelle*, April 1915

There is a place in Belgium where Europe's history can be sensed rather than seen. Neither cathedral nor monument, but just a simple grass verge immediately before the N253 decants its traffic into the arterial motorways of northern Europe.

At dawn, the morning chorus drowns the occasional putter of a car exhaust and the mists, tinged pink by the rising sun, pour down the rolling landscape to the west and gather in the valley below. As they curl and twist into spectral shapes, the cries of the wounded and the ghosts of the slain rise in poignant requiem. The spirits of countless generations are assembling – from the plains of Mons and Cambrai in front and the fields of Waterloo behind. A further twenty-five kilometres to the east is the centre of a political force whose *raison d'être* is to end wars in Europe forever – the city of Brussels.

Just below the ridge, lying hidden in the woods, is a small village that has known conflicts for centuries – a tranquil place of elegant villas surrounded by high walls and dense hedges. Only the wealthy live here for only they can pay for their expensive protection.

Secluded though his villa was, one owner could instantly communicate with every point in his global web and, like a self-satisfied spider, spent his days – waiting. There were two telephones on his desk: one for outgoing calls, the other for incoming ones. But few people had the number and they only dared call when matters were urgent.

One morning in the autumn of 1998 this telephone rang. The Spider let it ring twice, then picked up the receiver, but said nothing.

'This is Henri – calling from Paris.'

'You have *th*omething to *th*ay?' He cursed an impediment he could never cure.

Fluent in eight languages, he lisped in them all.

'There'll shortly be a press release. There's a new Agriculture Commissioner. Charles Marais. He's French.'

Henri waited – and waited. Finally a question came.

'*Ith* he amenable?' The last one certainly wasn't.

Henri swore quietly. To tell the Spider the truth or what he would like to hear. So as always, he hedged.

'He's very much his own man. The family's from the Auvergne – a stubborn, bloody-minded, independent lot.'

The Spider considered. Marais might not be amenable, but he was almost certainly vulnerable.

'You will find out everything.'

His flat assertion was all the more sinister for being spoken without a trace of feeling.

Brussels or no Brussels, in some form or other the conflicts continue.

CHAPTER TWO

The Ground, the Books, the Academes

From women's eyes this doctrine I derive;
They are the ground, the books, the academes,
From whence doth spring the true Promethean fire.

Shakespeare: *Love's Labour's Lost*

When, two months later, Dr Emma Austen took a call from
Brussels, conflicts were the last thing on her mind. Working
away on the computer, auburn hair gathered behind her
ears and faint lines of frowning concentration bisecting her
forehead, she was a picture of professional competence –
pretty too – and just thirty-two years old. Though presently
preoccupied with completing a report for a pharmaceutical
company, she was more generally consolidating her
consultancy firm, Components, that two years before she
had founded in Cambridge with her friend, Jane Acton.

'Madame Austen?' queried a man's voice.

'Speaking.'

'Good morning. My name is Arthos Danet and I'm in the
cabinet of Commissioner Charles Marais...'

Emma quickly disengaged her brain from medical matters
and re-engaged it in what she hoped was a Brussels mode.
New Commissioner she decided. She'd read about the
appointment some time ago.

'He's Agriculture – DG VI – isn't he?' she said.

4

'Yes, DG VI. Madame Austen, would it be possible for you to come to Brussels to meet the Commissioner? He wants a report on the beef crisis.'

Emma kept her brain firmly engaged in a Brussels mode. Why ever this, it objected? The European Court will take years to decide whether the French can continue to ban British beef. But this was no time to raise objections: Components needed all the work it could get.

'I'd be delighted. When would you like me to come?'

'As soon as possible, please. Next week?'

Emma picked up her diary and flipped the pages. 'The beginning is better for me than the end,' she volunteered.

In Brussels, Arthos scanned the Commissioner's diary. Wednesday was out, for that was the day the College – as the collective of Commissioners call themselves – held their sacrosanct weekly meeting. Monday too was out, for then the Commissioners' *chefs de cabinet* held *their* weekly meeting – just as sacrosanct, completely secret and far more influential. 'How about Tuesday morning, at 11.30?'

'That's fine.'

'Good. You'll come by Eurostar, I imagine? Please take a first-class ticket. I'll e-mail you details of how to find us.'

Emma was smiling as she replaced the receiver, remembering her initiation, several years back, into the bureaucracy of Brussels. She'd been asked to write a report for DG XII – Research and Development – a very timely job even though the signed contract only arrived eight weeks after she had completed the work and her invoice was not settled for months. For Components' sake she hoped their procedures had speeded up by now.

Still one was prepared to put up with quite a lot for profitable business. Though their business was now viable, the firm was not yet totally secure. A major contract would be highly welcome, being a foot in the door, money in the bank and potential for the future. She turned her PC off and went across to Jane's office to share the news.

The door was open and as she heard Emma's footsteps, Jane looked up and smiled.

'Surely it's too early for lunch?' she volunteered.

'Not really,' Emma replied. 'I think we've got a job.'

'Give me a couple of minutes. I'm almost through.'

Jane too, had spent the morning struggling with the pharmaceutical contract – analysing worksheets, preparing invoices and posting cheques to the stable of graduates who had helped them with research.

While she scribbled, Emma contemplated her friend – forty-one, happily married with two children approaching university age. They had known each other since childhood and were totally different. Jane knew that Emma's skills – in science, law and writing – were at the heart of Components' success, and that though dangerously impulsive at times, she had the vision necessary to take the company forward. Far from resenting these facts, Jane welcomed them. She contributed calm management and, in relishing the pernickety details Emma hated, never missed a trick with a contract.

Finally, Jane swung her chair away from the spreadsheets.

'Tell me.'

'Brussels.'

'Oh God.' said Jane involuntarily, and then laughed. 'No, I didn't really mean that. But getting to grips with their system can be excruciating. You know, it's not too early for a drink after all.'

Out in the minuscule square at the top of Portugal Place, they turned right down towards Jesus Green.

'Mitre, or Baron of Beef, or Rat and Parrot?' asked Jane.

'Don't let's bother with a pub. It's still warm. Let's have sandwiches outside.'

Though long shadows were already cast on the grass and the leaves had begun to change, Jesus Green was beautiful and they settled on a bench in the sunshine.

'Now tell me.'

'But one thing puzzles me,' Emma said finally. 'Why a report on beef when we're all in limbo?'

'Don't even ask. We'll find out soon enough. Besides, Ned'll probably pick up some gossip when he's next in Brussels.'

Ned was Jane's brilliant husband – a peripatetic economist and regular consultant to the Commission and many European governments.

'And this time round you'll probably come to love the bureaucracy.'

'Care to bet?'

Her report safely despatched, Emma left the office, walked along the south edge of Jesus Green, crossed over at Four Lamps roundabout and on towards The Kite and New Square. Usually she faced a cold Cambridge gale, but today was glorious warm air and a gentle breeze that blew her silk scarf across her face. She crossed diagonally over the Green to the south side of New Square and her tiny end-terrace house.

She ran upstairs, slipped into jeans and a green sweater then took a quick walk around the garden to smell the roses. Back in the sitting-room she poured a single malt whisky, switched on the hi-fi, settled into a comfortable chair and decided that life was finally coming good.

Six years and several disastrous episodes ago, she had wondered. But being a natural survivor, she had regrouped and started to carve out a successful career. Still, she now took great care to preserve her autonomy. Attractive and highly competent, she was widely respected and mostly loved though some people loathed her – too successful by half! Still, she had a wide circle of friends and was finding Cambridge fascinating. But she had ring-fenced herself. If life was lonely at times, so be it. She would avoid any situation likely to shatter the security she had so carefully built. But there'll be no danger of that with this job, she reflected – so orderly and regulated was the cautious Commission. There the status quo certainly ruled OK. So going to the telephone she booked a seat on Eurostar and then a hotel in Brussels.

CHAPTER THREE

Wandering on a Foreign Strand

*But the political decision, the most extreme option open to the Minister,
was made on the basis of a questionable scientific paper, following the
deliberations of a committee offering advice in a climate where scientific
advisors are asked to behave in highly political ways and where politicians,
in perpetual fear of the media, become spin doctors. The Tories handled
BSE by suppressing scientific advice. Cunningham, [Labour UK Minister for
Agriculture, 1997] barely paused to consider it.
Both outcomes represent a victory of politics over science.*

'Another Casualty in the Beef War?' Emily Green: *New Statesman*,
12th December 1997, p.32

One week later Emma was en route for Brussels. Dressed in
a lightweight, mushroom-coloured skirt and jacket, a simple
gold ornament on the lapel, cream silk blouse and another
of her many coloured silk scarves, she looked happy and
successful. Her shoulder-length hair, lightly bleached by
the summer sun, spilled attractively over her collar. When
the seasons changed it would revert to a darker colour. Her
green eyes were as soft as a fawn's; a small, anticipatory
smile was playing around her mouth. The steward, who
served a singularly disappointing lunch for first-class
passengers, regularly returned for several more looks.

Someone is a lucky sod! he thought.

As the taxi swung out of the Gare du Midi, Emma's first
glimpses of the city were not endearing. When not grey and

drab, the buildings were beige and drab – modern concrete blocks run up in a hurry. But once in the Place Stéphanie, both atmosphere and architecture improved. Several streets fanned out from the circle and one – the Avenue Louise – became an elegant boulevard flanked by leafy trees and an old-fashioned tramline that stretched away up the hill. However, in the side-streets it was back to beige concrete blocks again. But the hotel was clean and the staff friendly.

Next morning she called for a taxi.

'Where to, Madame?' The driver spoke in French and she answered in French.'To Breydel, please.'

'Ah, the Commission,' and they swept off through another landscape of uninspiring buildings. Ten minutes later he turned into the Avenue d'Auderghem, then down a narrow street towards an arc of tall posts carrying fifteen European national flags – that marked the Commission's headquarters. But the entrance road was blocked by traffic cones and a stolid security man, so the driver stopped some way from the main doors.

'You must get out here,' he said firmly.

Emma walked briskly through one set of glass doors, teetered over a covered forecourt of cobbled stones and through more glass doors into the lobby. At reception a severe looking lady graciously inclined her head.

'Good morning. I'm Emma Austen. I have an appointment with Commissioner Marais at 11.30. My contact is Monsieur Arthos Danet.'

'Very good. You will give me your passport, please?' This was a command, not a request.

'Someone will be down shortly. Kindly take a seat.' But being a creature of insatiable curiosity, Emma took a walk instead.

Up on the seventh floor, Charles Marais was rounding off a meeting with his *cabinet*, when his secretary came in: 'Commissioner, Dr Austen has arrived.'

'Very good. We've just about finished. Arthos, will you go and receive our visitor please?'

Arthos' exit was a general signal that the meeting was over. As his *cabinet* collected their papers, Marais regarded them thoughtfully. A newcomer was about to enter their lives. He knew they would be polite but could guarantee neither their co-operation nor their friendliness, for he remembered the fury that had erupted when he had lobbed his grenade into their midst. He had only been in the job for a short time yet quickly found himself in a first-class row.

'I want an independent report on all aspects of the BSE crisis as it affected us from day one.'

The appalled silence was broken by his shocked *chef de cabinet*, Dr Felice Fede, an Italian who had been in Brussels through the reigns of several Agriculture Commissioners.

Widely known as 'FF', Fede's name literally translated as 'happy belief'. Unfortunately, it combined the first name of one notoriously corrupt Italian with the family name of another – equally notorious and corrupt. Fede reacted apopletically to the use of his initials.

He didn't fit the stereotype of a cheerful, spontaneous Italian, for he was orthodox and very formal. Imaginative flexibility was not part of his nature and Fede played strictly by the bureaucratic rules, and always managed to balance on the fence, even if somewhat precariously. But, as Fede had recognised from the start of his career, this was a huge advantage: he could never be blamed if things went wrong.

Now he shot the cuffs of his expensive shirt. 'Of course, Commissioner, if that is your wish. But permit me to ask. Surely this is not necessary?'

'I believe it is,' replied Marais. 'The British have conducted a wide-ranging enquiry and it could be instructive for us to do the same.'

'Commissioner,' the German deputy *chef*, Willi Dashöfer, spoke next, as protocol dictated. 'I must protest most strongly. I believe this decision to be most unwise.'

Willi Dashöfer had also been 'inherited', for knowing that his own term would be short, Marais decided to retain four of his predecessor's *cabinet*. Fifty-five years old, medium height, Dashöfer was solidly built, with grey hair and a curiously reddish beard which was not always neatly trimmed. Extremely competent, his attitude was as unyielding as his frame and Marais found him difficult to gauge. But he did know that in contravention of all Commission rules, Dashöfer maintained close contact with his government in Berlin.

Marais made no comment. I know why you are saying this he thought. Germany still doesn't want to take British beef.

Dashöfer went on, 'May I ask your reasons?'

'Well, this crisis never seems to end. When we banned the export of Portuguese beef, Isabel Cunha, a Portuguese journalist wrote in *O Público* that there was no point Portugal crying "It's not fair". For when the beef crisis was underway, Britain then, like Portugal now, was not given a fair hearing, but went ahead and stamped out the disease. She suggests the Portuguese should stop whingeing and do the same. Were the British not given a fair hearing?'

'Of course, they were,' objected Dashöfer. 'Every single decision throughout was taken on strictly scientific grounds. Her suggestion is outrageous.'

Marais longed to comment 'you could have fooled me', but instead turned to the third person in his *cabinet* to have been in the Commission for years. Céline Bardot, who came from Nice, made no attempt to hide her nostalgia for the earlier days, when to be young was very heaven. Idealistic, conscientious, her countenance permanently tinged with anxiety, she was the quintessential Red Queen, always running hard to stay in the same place. But bright as a button, she could cut clean through bureaucratic verbiage in a trice and go straight to the heart of an issue. Though short, plump and wearing unflattering spectacles, she dressed well but simply, her wardrobe causing neither surprise nor delight.

'Commissioner,' Céline brushed back her hair from her face as she spoke. 'When independent reports are requested there is always one problem.'

'And that is?' encouraged Marais.

'Access to our files. They are highly confidential.'

'If we find someone well-qualified to do this job I shall instruct you to give them the necessary access.'

Now the storm really broke. Their new boss was threatening to be an uncontrollable cannon. Céline looked desperately unhappy, Dashöfer was protesting loudly, so Fede, praying that a fresh explanation would make his Commissioner see reason, stepped in once more.

'Commissioner,' his voice was pleading as he shot his cuffs. 'You must understand that matters are never conducted in this way. If external reports are deemed necessary – and they rarely are – then a group of sound and trusted specialists must be commissioned. All points of view must be properly represented. If you need seven different background papers on this issue, then we will be happy to commission seven different consultants to prepare them.'

Still as a heron, right hand supporting chin, index finger running up cheek-bone, Marais listened intently. But his impatience was obvious.

'Look, I'm thoroughly fed up with the huge army of permanent advisors who discuss only the things that fascinate them, who see all the trees but not the wood and abandon us completely when it comes to an overall synthesis.'

The German's red beard positively bristled. 'Commissioner, you cannot do this. The Commission does not conduct business in this way.'

'I can and maybe it's time for a change.'

Marais caught the look that passed between his *chef* and his deputy – the Latin's shrug, the German's glare. They had a loose cannon on their hands, all right.

He now turned to Sybilla Høgstrøm. She had first appeared in the *cabinet* four years back, being paid for by a Danish government department. Such outsiders are known as *sousmarins* (submarines) and are 'invisible' – not registered on the Commission's book. Many quietly manoeuvred through the bureaucratic channels, then suddenly surfaced to capture a permanent plum job. So they were greatly resented by the established staff.

She was also Marais' mistress. They had been on a mission to Piedmont. Marais' presence was not really necessary, but he had been pinned to his desk for weeks. In any case he had wanted to see things for himself – not just receive reports refracted through the prism of Italian national self-interest. The trip was exhausting – too many meetings, too many functions. On the second day a special lunch was laid on – a lengthy occasion of food, wine, liqueurs. He had struggled between the demands of good manners and his trim figure. That night he had felt exceedingly unwell so, with flushed and swollen face, retired early. Sybilla followed to see if he needed help and for the next twenty-four hours supported him through his sickness.

Back in Brussels he accepted with detached gratitude what Sybilla clearly wanted to offer, sliding smoothly into the tranquillity of her cool embrace. His emotions, however, were not engaged. They probably never would be again, for his beloved wife of thirty years had died only nine months before. The affair was conducted with discreet dignity and to his everlasting gratitude she made no demands at all – neither flaunting the relationship nor seeking advantage from it.

Sousmarin she might be, but Marais reckoned most people found it difficult to resent Sybilla for she was intelligent and debonair, with a sparkling personality that could diffuse tense moments with irreverent humour. She might have been a touch too dismissive of subordinates, but had none of the aggressive toughness associated with many Nordic maidens and danced the minuets of the Commission's procedures with flair and assurance. Gossip said she came from an exceedingly wealthy, aristocratic Danish background. Certainly she dressed as if she did, with outfits that constantly surprised and delighted.

Now she bestowed a mischievous smile on the entire *cabinet*. She was going to disagree with Fede and Dashöfer and enjoy every minute.

'Of course we should do this. Though I am not at all sure about how we go about finding someone suitable.'

Marais next turned to the three energetic young Frenchmen he had brought with him to Brussels. They were very different from the rest of the *cabinet*. For them, Europe was not a vision – merely a job – a useful rung on their career ladder en route to a major political post back home.

Almost in unison, but not quite, the three nodded in agreement.

Finally, Marais turned to his Director-General, Charles Stewart, tall, British, laconic, supercompetent, with an in-furiating self-assured politeness.

'Commissioner, I have a suggestion. There's an outfit in Cambridge called Components that could do a good job. Its President, Dr Emma Austen, did scientific research for a while, then became a lawyer.'

'Might she not be a little too like Margaret Thatcher?' observed Céline. 'It would hardly be appropriate for her to have access to our files?'

There was a general laugh around the table and Arthos muttered under his breath, 'Where is that famous handbag now we need it?'

'Tell me more,' invited Marais.

'Well, she started up this consultancy company that deals with every aspect of science save laboratory research. They're becoming very successful. I know about her because she did a super job a few years ago. DG XII needed a comprehensive report on Japanese molecular biology, along with a three-page summary for EU politicians on the run...'

'I take it you mean in a hurry?'

'Indeed.' Stewart grinned, grateful for a boss with a sense of humour and an understanding of English nuances.

'Dr Austen's efforts were very well-regarded. Her report came in on time, on budget and on target. The Commission didn't settle her bill for months, though!'

'We shall have to do better,' and Marais nodded towards Céline.

There wasn't all that much for Emma to see. To the left of the reception desk a gilded display in blue and gold, extolled the virtues of the euro. To the right, was a large photograph of the acting Commissioners seated around their red-topped table. Emma wondered how many she could identify. Her score was, she decided, quite deplorable. The men looked distinctly smug; the five women mischievous. What a difference from the last – indeed the only time Emma had seen them all together, when their self-satisfied smirks were well and truly wiped from their faces. They were being filmed for the evening news, while anxiously watching the debate in the European Parliament on television monitors. The furious Parliamentarians were on the verge of passing a resolution of no confidence on the whole group, on the grounds of fraud, corruption, incompetence and nepotism – and that was just for starters. No wonder the Commissioners had looked glum: most were soon to be out of a lovely job.

She heard a gentle cough behind her.

'Madame Austen?'

Emma turned to face a young man of about twenty-five, medium height, dark eyes in a face that while it reflected energetic intelligence, appeared squashed. It was the nose, she finally decided, broken – whilst skiing or perhaps playing rugby? But he was far too small to have been in the scrum and wasn't lithe enough to be a wing three-quarter. Perhaps he'd had a fist-fight. He was grinning cheerfully and she liked him at once.

'You must be Arthos Danet?' she asked as they shook hands.

'Yes, Madame Austen. I am one of the Three Musketeers in Commissioner Marais' *cabinet*.'

'One of the what?'

'He brought us three gallant Frenchmen to serve with him in the College.'

'Then it figures.' Emma said smilingly, as he steered her towards the security desk.

'I can't offer to take your briefcase until you have successfully negotiated that device,' Arthos said, pointing to the right.

As he followed the sign labelled *'Badges'* and *'Magnétiques'*; she went towards *'Visitors'* and *'Visiteurs'*, and through the electronic rectangle under the careful scrutiny of a guard, to emerge unscathed at the other side.

Now Arthos reached for her briefcase.

'Your first visit to Brussels, Madame Austen?'

'Yes.'

'Well, I'm a newcomer too.'

'Did you Musketeers know each other before you came?'

'No, not really, though two of us already had a reputation in the Elysée Palace.'

For political acumen rather than fisticuffs, she thought, as Arthos held back the lift door.

'We're meeting in the Commissioner's private office on the seventh floor and I've allowed forty-five minutes for our discussion. Then Céline Bardot – another French *cabinet* member who's been here forever – will show you round. I've set up a meeting with our contract people at 2.30. But in between, perhaps you would care to take lunch with me and the other Musketeers?'

'I'm game for anything.' Emma warmed to this lively, laconic young man.

As she went in through the door of the Commissioner's office – a spacious room, large antique desk, sofa, armchairs, and a low table on which coffee was already placed – Marais was signing some letters. Her eyes were drawn first to him and then to a photograph on the desk against which was propped a postcard of a medieval painting. Marais rose at once.

She saw a man, probably sixty years old, but who looked younger, of medium height, thin, grey hair crowning an oval, sculpted face, with fine bone structure. He had a disarming smile, but though there were laughter lines at the corners of the eyes, there was an underlying sadness in his look. What really struck her was the sense of calm repose: there's something formidable here, she thought, and she liked what she saw.

Marais bent over her hand.

'Madame Austen.'

I'm going to have to get used to this mode of address, she realised.

'Thank you for coming.' He stepped back. He saw a slim, elegant woman, early thirties, simply dressed in a long tailored skirt and jacket made of soft swirling fabrics, set off by a stunning silk scarf. She had an excellent complexion, light make-up skilfully applied, and an air that combined expectancy and competence. But there's a strength here, he concluded; she'd been through the fire. He liked what he saw.

'May I introduce Dr Felice Fede, my *chef de cabinet*.'

Fede bowed over her hand too. 'Welcome to the Commission, Madame Austen.'

'Dr Willi Dashöfer.'

Emma shook the hand of the tall florid man whose skin was faintly moist to the touch. He was trying not to glare, she decided. 'Madame Austen' was all he said.

'Céline Bardot, who has been a long-time pillar of strength in the Commission.'

As Céline stepped forward, her right hand brushed back her hair.

'I'm glad to meet you.'

'And Arthos you have met.'

Marais indicated a chair to his left and they all sat down.

'There are two things I would like you to do, Madame Austen,' he began. 'First, I need a series of papers on certain aspects of the BSE crisis. These I shall circulate to all the European Agricultural Ministers as well as members of our two Veterinary Committees and the Scientific Advisory Committee. Then I will convene a day's meeting when you will present your conclusions for discussion. Though they won't all come, I hope that after this exercise we will be better equipped to handle future crises.'

'You think they will occur?' queried Emma.

'They already have. Both France and Germany retain bans on UK beef. BSE is more widespread in Europe than we've admitted and may well be present in North America and Australia. The Portuguese think it's unfair that we've slapped a ban on their beef. But what constitutes fairness in such a situation? I sense that as the BSE crisis evolved, matters became more convoluted and I'm not convinced that appropriate decisions were taken. Come to that, I'm not even convinced that we've a true grasp of the science.'

The room was comfortably warm, but Emma swore she could see frost particles forming on Fede's nose and Dashöfer's beard.

'So I want you to look into these matters for us. I want to know how public perceptions were fashioned; how decisions were taken and with what rationale – scientific, political or by default; what mistakes you think were made, by whom, and when, and with what consequences; and how might similar ones be avoided in the future?'

He waited deliberately. If Dr Austen was any good, she would have questions.

'Commissioner, we will be comprehensive of course, but may we state the unthinkable should the need arise?'

Chin supported by right hand, Marais watched her intently. Now he smiled: 'You need not trouble to wrap up unpleasant truths in diplomatic niceties.'

Thank God, thought Emma. That's one problem out of the way.

'My second point is even more crucial, for it concerns the conditions under which my company is willing to undertake such reports. What access may we have to people and files?'

'I've already decided that you are to see whatever files you wish. Céline will be responsible for accommodating you.'

But Emma noticed that even as Céline Bardot nodded assent, she was looking distinctly troubled, while Fede looked positively mortified.

'Finally,' said Marais, ignoring all the negative vibes, 'I assume that you personally will be responsible for this assignment.'

'Of course.'

'Well, that's settled.' said Marais and gave her his wonderful smile. 'This is not the first time you've done a report for the Commission, is it?'

'No, Commissioner, though last time I didn't actually have to visit Brussels.'

'Well, I hope our procedures have improved since then. Céline will facilitate all matters – whether contracts or payments.'

God, he's been well briefed, thought Emma admiringly.

'So I look forward to seeing a great deal of you in the coming months. Please feel free to discuss anything with me at any time.'

He rose and again bent over her hand.

As Emma left the private office with Céline, she heard Marais say, 'Arthos, there was a tragic incident in DG VI some years back. The Quatraro affair. I want to know everything about it.'

Now who the hell was Quatraro, thought Emma, as she went through the door. I don't recognise the name.

The lunch with the Three Musketeers was short and jolly, though there was something that puzzled her: in some way or other, Arthos was different from the others.

By contrast, the meeting with the contract and finance officers was prolonged and serious. But by half past three she was free so decided to explore, and to her surprised delight realised that there were treasures to discover in Brussels and two were close by her hotel. The square and church of Parvis de la Trinité – an exquisite vignette of baroque architecture – lay at the end of a small bustling side street off Avenue Louise.

Then swinging back down the boulevard, hair blowing in the breeze, scanning the elegant shops as she went, she passed Les Enfants d'Edouard, whose window display proclaimed *'Haute Couture'*. Emma shook her head: way beyond her budget. But ten yards further on her mind registered what her eyes had seen – a card that said *'Secondhand Clothes'*. She swung round, dived in and emerged half an hour later with a cashmere coat that beautifully accommodated both her figure and her bank balance. At that moment Emma decided she might well enjoy Brussels after all.

CHAPTER FOUR

Sweetness and Light

Scientific terrorism takes the following form. You isolate a small quantity of statistic, attach it to a lengthy fuse of language, and leave it in a public place for a politician to trip over. More disreputable practitioners then telephone a message to the press, demanding a large sum of money for 'more research' to be deposited in a named University.

Simon Jenkins: *The Times*, 4th September 1998

'To be honest, I'm still appallingly ignorant about the Commission,' Emma admitted, forty-eight hours later. 'And in any case I have a love-hate relationship.'

'Join the club.' Ned dipped his fingers into the saucepan and licked them. 'More garlic.'

She was with Jane and Ned in their converted barn in Elmdon, a village eight miles south of Cambridge. Ned was cooking pasta sauce, Jane making the salad, while Emma, sitting with a glass of Argentinian Malbec in her hand, was feeling deliciously irresponsible.

'I've seen it all,' Ned rubbed his nose.

An unusual academic, reflected Emma, looking at the stocky, fair-haired figure. He didn't just stay in an ivory tower thinking up great ideas, but got directly involved in practical action to realise them.

'I've seen it all,' he repeated. 'The Commission's a hard-working bureaucratic juggernaut, full of well-meaning people for the most part, who spend weeks discussing what views they must consider before they dare act. But always I get the feeling...'

'That...?' As Jane tossed the salad Emma caught the light fleetingly reflected in the oil on the leaves.

Ned dipped his fingers into the sauce once more.

'Much better! ...they are certain they know what's best for me. Even better than I do. They're all the same, especially the *énarques*. I bet your Commissioner's *cabinet* is stuffed full of them.'

Emma choked on her wine. 'Stuffed full of what?'

'Graduates of the French *Ecole Nationale d'Administration*.'

Emma took a proper slurp. 'Are they important?'

'Are they ever. Of the hundred and fifty who emerge each year, ten per cent are very bright indeed, ten per cent just so-so, the rest merely competent. But no matter: they all go into the very top jobs. They've inhabited every nook and cranny of the Commission from the start. If you're one you surround yourself with others and why? Because you know they can be trusted to take the right decisions on behalf of everybody else.'

His voice was light, but there was no mistaking the irony.

'Pretend you don't like them,' teased Jane. 'How would you describe them now?'

'In a very pointed manner. Nerds in double-breasted suits, carrying red boxes, spending other people's money.' Ned grinned. 'And,' he turned to Emma, 'in case you think I'm being deplorably chauvinistic, these are not my words but those of French students. They've formed a new political party and called for another Bastille Day with a revolution against the aristocracy of the *énarques*. They haven't a hope in hell, but possibly something is getting through...'

Emma suddenly guessed why Arthos seemed different from the other Musketeers. She'd bet he wasn't an *énarque*.

'...because this year's graduates wrote to Jospin, demanding the government do something about the College's image. They're worried that not only are they regarded as impossibly arrogant, but blamed for France's lousy economic performance.'

He strained the pasta and started to ladle out sauce. Jane was laughing.

'Let's eat. Em, I've gone through the papers you brought back. The budget is giving me the usual headache. It's not straightforward but perfectly possible. Have you ever heard of units?'

'Only in kitchens. What are they?'

'Well, a unit can be a month's work for a full-time person, or a week's work for a part-time one, or ten computers, or ten thousand telephone calls – anything you like in fact, so long as the bureaucrats can be kept happy adding them up.'

Emma's irreverent streak declared itself. 'So let's keep them happy, then. A unit is one journalist's misrepresentation of fact, or one row between two vets discussing BSE. I bet I'm going to find a quantifiable amount of both.'

'The Commission won't pay you for those.'

'Not fair – the journalists and vets got paid.'

Jane and Ned raised their glasses.

'To units.'

'Anyway,' Jane continued, 'that's one thing. Another is that I've already lined up three graduate students for you to interview. One is especially well-qualified. He'd done his homework and volunteered a gem on science terrorism.'

Ned spoke again but there was no lightness in his voice.

'Em – you must remember that not all is sweetness and light in DG VI.'

'How come?'

'Its reputation for fraud and mismanagement is second to none. I'd bet even money your Commissioner has a hidden agenda in bringing you in.'

Emma suddenly stopped eating as Marais' last words flashed into her mind.

'Ned, what was the Quatraro affair?'

Ned gazed at her in mock admiration. 'How did you learn about that?'

'I heard Commissioner Marais ask Arthos Danet to find out everything about it. I'm curious.'

'You always were. Well, it's possibly the most infamous scandal in Agriculture. Tragic, certainly. It's in the public domain. Antonio Quatraro was an Italian staff member, who went up to the top of the building and jumped off.'

'My God! Or was he pushed?'

'What a suspicious mind you've got. Depends who you ask. Suicide was possible, for he was facing public disgrace. On the other hand, he was involved with an Italian scam and organised crime, so rumours were flying all over the place that someone was settling accounts.'

'What do you believe?'

'Find it hard to know what to believe. Now he's dead it is extremely difficult to work out what happened. But had UCLAF – the Commission's anti-fraud squad – been able to prove criminal activity, he could well have gone to gaol.'

'What was the scam?' Jane too, was intrigued.

'Well, it starts with the fact that the tobacco produced in the Community is so awful that no one wants it. But huge sums of money were sloshing around DG VI covering a mountain of subsidies – for farmers to grow it, for processors to buy it and export subsidies to help sell it, as well as grants for others, in Albania mostly, to burn it. At that time tobacco subsidies were thirty-five times bigger than those for wheat.'

'What time?'

'Between 1987 and 1990. He didn't jump till '93.'

'Who got all the lovely money?'

'Greece and Italy tapped a whopping eighty per cent.'

Emma was riveted.

'Phew!'

'Eat up. Now Quatraro was head of a division responsible both for regulating the tobacco crop and doling out the huge subsidies for dumping it.'

'Ned, you should be thoroughly ashamed,' observed Emma severely, 'I suspect that in Brussels "dumping" is a politically most incorrect term.'

'Too right. They prefer to say "disposing of surpluses". So Quatraro's pals collected the subsidies, while he took a cut of some 1.2 million dollars.'

'Why would he want all that money?'

'Why would he not want it? He'd been secretary of the Christian Democratic Party's office in Brussels for four years and insisted the money went there. How innocent, I hear you say, except when you remember that the Head of the Christian Democratic Party at that time – one of Italy's Prime Ministers, no less – was found to have had close links with the Mafia for years.'

'If he hadn't jumped, would he have been picked up?'

'Well, to an extent he already had. Accusations were flying all over the place, but – same old story – for far too long the Commission imposed a total press blackout and did bloody nothing. Even the enquiries they ultimately started insisted nothing untoward had occurred and Quatraro lost his job only after several months. Even then he was offered early retirement on a pension I'd happily accept. He refused and was shunted sideways. But the rumours never died down.'

'How was he shopped?'

'A complaint from rivals of his Italian pals started the investigation. Remember Em, this case was one very important reason why the Parliamentarians became interested in internal fraud and corruption in the first place. They knew the Commission had suppressed the story.'

'What other scams are going on?'

'Quite a few. I'll lend you a book – *Main Basse sur l'Europe* – by François d'Aubert.

'*The Mugging of Europe,*' said Emma, 'What a delicious title.'

Ned now turned serious. 'You're going to hate me but I have a suggestion. If you feel as ignorant as you make out, there's only one person in Cambridge you should talk to.'

'Oh, no,' said Emma with real feeling. She knew only too well, the bullying, lascivious, but irresistibly entertaining, Sir Robert Partridge.

'Oh, yes,' insisted Ned.

'No please, I'm not that ignorant – really!'

'But you are!'

'Close your eyes and think of Components.' Jane intervened. 'We need the work.'

'He's at St Peter's almost every night,' Ned went on, '...and since I know the Master, it's not going to be difficult for me to wangle an invitation.'

'Quite so,' they said and lifted their glasses again. 'Enjoy the dinner.'

'Damn you,' laughed Emma. 'You did this on purpose.'

CHAPTER FIVE

The Pillars of the Temple

When he had made scourge of small cords,
he drove them all out of the temple

The Bible: Gospel According to St John 2:15

Thank heaven they suggested St Peter's. There was safety in numbers. Partridge's home would be one sacrifice too far. So she called her old tutor, Sir Alexander Gough, President of The Royal Society, and so distinguished that the Fellows of St Peter's – all renowned arts scholars – had no qualms in electing a scientist as their Master.

'I understand your winsome ways well,' said Gough. 'Who do you want to sit next to?'

When Emma told him, the reply was swift, 'I don't believe it. Not for his blue eyes, surely?'

'No, indeed. We've a job to do in Brussels.'

'How about next Tuesday; 7.15?'

Thus one week after her meeting with Marais, Emma was in the company of Sir Robert Partridge who, as a young man, had walked the Brussels corridors of power. He was on secondment to the Commissioner for the Internal Market - a Conservative who had actually been sent to Brussels by a Labour Prime Minister, Harold Wilson. But while his boss had a made a real impact, Partridge had not. So he flew back to academe.

Waspish and brilliant, Partridge was both a disgruntled don and a disillusioned diplomat, having achieved neither fame nor success in either field, but only stacks of money – how, no one was sure. He was also sad, vain and lonely, with impulses in no way diminished by the passage of time. Emma found him alternately fascinating and repellent, a person whose sophisticated intellect was matched by a grossness in his appearance and sexual approaches.

Not that it would matter how subtle his approaches, thought Emma. I can't stand him.

Still, St Peter's provided more than adequate compensation. She loved its settled antiquity, the exquisite panelled hall dating back to 1290. The gathering in the Combination Room was small that evening. Only a few Fellows and one other guest were standing around the burnished pie-crust table in front of the fireplace.

Partridge was enchanted to see her. She would be next to him at dinner. Then coffee and brandy would follow and who knows what else? Even if he were no longer young, the night certainly was.

'My dearest Emma,' he spluttered and made to kiss her lips. But she moved her face smartly to the right and presented her left cheek. 'And we are sitting together and I am no fool – you want something.'

'There's no hurry,' murmured Emma vaguely, already disconcerted.

'Oh, but there is. Time's winged chariot, don't you know? You have been in Brussels, I hear? And you are going there again.'

God Almighty, thought Emma, how did he know?

'Actually, I wanted your opinion on the beef crisis.'

'That piddling little episode. That stupid irrelevance. That trivial disturbance on the vast tides of German–French destiny. Europe's patterns are too firmly fixed for that to have any effect whatsoever.'

'Why?'

'Do you have no sense of history, my dear girl? But there, how could you? You were not alive at the Creation. You saw the light of day in...?'

'1968,' said Emma shortly.

'One must go back years before to find an answer to your why. Consider, I implore you, the consequences of two world wars.'

Then, to Emma's surprise, his face drooped and his voice became sad.

'Consider them. They were shattering, for us in Britain, because two generations of our young men had died and we were exhausted and flat broke. Shattering too, for our enemies, Germany, and our betrayers, France. And it seemed the pattern would persist indefinitely.'

As she listened, Emma became troubled. Perhaps she was insensitive. Who did he once love, she wondered. Had anyone ever loved him?

'That I do know – and the only way to break the pattern was by establishing fresh alliances.'

'Clever girl. But who in their right mind would start a political alliance with Germany? No one at all.'

'So what did they do?' queried Emma.

'I will tell you at dinner.'

The Master collected everyone with his eye. 'Shall we go in?'

He went directly to his high-backed chair, unusually not in the middle of the High Table, but at one end. Emma was in the centre under the gaze of an earlier Master, Edmund Keene, Bishop of Chester and Ely, and the scientist, Lord Kelvin. Partridge slid behind her, right arm brushing her back as he moved. On her left was an earnest bespectacled don she had never met before.

Grace was said, wine poured, soup served, but Emma felt ill at ease, though couldn't understand why. Something to

31

do perhaps, with the uncomfortable feelings that many women in Cambridge currently experience in the presence of old-fashioned males in their old-fashioned Senior Common Rooms? But then realising that, as usual, Robert Partridge had disconcerted her, she allowed herself a bleak smile. Tossing her head like a sensitive horse, she chuckled at Jane's injunction 'close your eyes and think of Components', then turned back to Partridge, sweetly prepared to do her duty.

'You were saying that no one would establish a political alliance with Germany?'

'So I was. Politicians were desperate, for reconciliation had to start with the two traditional enemies, Germany and France. There was no alternative. Blessed St Margaret of Thatcher, where were you when we needed you?'

In spite of her unease, Emma began laughing. The Master caught her eye and winked.

'Enter Jean Monnet. Since the causes of war are economic not political, let economics become the tool. Harness the Ruhr's coal and steel for peace and so bind Germany in a permanent political union.'

'I'm not naïve,' said Emma, 'What did the French get in return?'

'Indeed you are not, my dearest Emma, for, as Mr Knightley so rightly said, "dearest you always will be whatever the event of this hour's conversation"...'

Emma knew her Jane Austen equally well and became impatient.

'Oh please get on.'

'If you insist, but you are a far nicer topic of conversation. By the way, this food is disgusting. I trust our College ghost is haunting the Bursar personally.'

Emma was surprised. She thought the meal rather good.

'What ghost?' She gazed down the hall but could see neither ectoplasm nor spectre, only eighteen small portraits on wood panels – earlier Masters, Fellows and benefactors. Did Partridge hope to be up there with them one day? He was known to have lavished funds on the college.

'One Francis Dawes – Bursar in 1789. He hanged himself with a bell-rope.'

'Why?'

'For allegedly – they always say allegedly do they not, in these grossly litigious times – tampering with the election of the Master. How appropriate – now we are discussing Brussels, my dear. Corruption, cronyism in high places – a deeply, dishonourable lot.'

'Are you referring to dead dons of St Peter's or living bureaucrats in Brussels?'

'I find it hard to distinguish. But I digress. The quid pro quo was breathtakingly simple. If the French would open their markets to the industries of the Ruhr – which they had always refused to do – the Germans would forever pay and French farmers forever be protected from all market forces.'

'Enter the Common Agricultural Policy – CAP for short – that still swallows most of the budget. But, of course, the French got a whole lot more besides – their system of governance for a start. Since the Germans felt guilty then – and continued to do so for the next fifty years – they gave the French everything they wanted. By the way Emma, undergraduates pay very high fees these days for tutorials. What price are you prepared to pay?'

'None at all.' said Emma with undisguised irritation.

'Ah, well. So the fruits of this indissoluble association were the Union and the Commission and all else that followed, including the many ineffectual Commissioners. Oh dear, oh dear! Bound together by laws of incestuous collegiality, they take all decisions behind closed doors. They reveal nothing to inquisitive and ignorant outsiders like you, who should know their place. They erect insurmountable barriers to any attempts to call them to

33

account. So who controls Brussels; who elects Brussels; who fires Brussels? Absolutely bloody no one.'

'But surely the elected Council of Ministers exerts democratic control over the Commission?' said Emma.

'No, it doesn't.'

'Why doesn't it?'

'My dear Emma, use that brilliant brain of yours, enclosed in that exquisite body! First, because its meetings are totally secret and second, it *cannot* be in charge.'

'Why ever not?'

'Because the Treaty of Rome insists that the Council must act on the proposals of the unelected Commission, yet cannot dictate to them. To do so would be to bring down the pillars of the Temple. So the Commissioners may be incompetent, corrupt, immoral, frivolous and territorial; they may take decisions based on bribes, nepotism, favouritism or sheer political expediency – all vices they manifest. Yet the Council cannot sack them.'

He sighed deeply. 'If I am going to continue with this tutorial I need more claret – much more claret. You too, need more claret.' He stretched out his arm for the decanter and filled her glass. 'If we both drink too much claret...'

'You're not very subtle,' observed Emma.

'How times have changed from the days of my youth. You didn't have to be subtle then.'

'Times have changed completely,' said Emma very firmly, 'You not only have to be subtle; you actually have to be nice.'

He turned and regarded her intently.

'There is a most unpleasant directness about you, my dear Emma, which could well have disqualified you from the attentions of the handsome young men in my time. The trouble is, I don't think you would have cared. Who is to blame? Germaine Greer?'

34

'Don't trouble to blame anyone,' said Emma as she sipped her claret. 'Just accept it.'

'If you insist. When, perish the thought, the Commission initiates an unwise, even a mistaken policy – which of course it never does, for it has argued endlessly about it beforehand – then bugger-all happens. No one will even admit the problem – for it is not in the nature of powerful bureaucrats in powerful positions ever to admit mistakes. Much easier to blame the Council of Ministers.'

'Do they deserve any blame?' queried Emma.

'To an extent. Though you would never guess it from Robin Cook and his spin doctors, their debates are perfunctory and ill-attended. Any Ministers who turn up, arrive exhausted and stay the shortest possible time. Others are famous for sleeping soundly throughout – shall I name them? – and at five o'clock, or whenever they wake up, all they want to do is to get back to bed – wherever bed is and whoever else is in it.

'Of course, Jacques Delors was devilishly clever. He managed to flatter both the Council of Ministers and the European Parliament into total acquiescence, while blithely pursuing his own agenda, armed with a whole stack of reputable reasons even when his ideas were patently wrong.'

'Oh, surely they never were?'

'I did not realize you could be so sarcastic. He felt it was the Commission's duty – under his guidance of course – to put forward revolutionary policies and would be astonished at any suggestion he was acting outside his remit. He'd quote the Treaty of Rome.'

'What about the voices of ordinary people like me?'

'Forget them. Such notions would never occur to Delors or any other *énarque*. Do you know what an *énarque* is?'

'Yes.'

'Then you should know what I'm talking about.'

'But what about the European Parliament?' said Emma faintly. God, she really was clutching at straws.

'What about it?'

'They nearly voted the Commissioners out.'

'There you go again – demonstrating your utter naïvity. What's significant is not that they nearly voted them out, but they didn't actually do so. Bloody wimps. They asked a Committee of Wise Men to investigate, but they found what the press found, what the Court of Auditors found, what the poor bloody whistle-blower – the only one to emerge with any credit – found. Whenever there's fraud, nepotism, malpractice, bribes or poor management, what happens? Bloody little. They growled like lions but acted like pussy-cats. They still can't sack any one individual.'

He turned to face her fully and for the first time she thought she saw the mask drop.

'Emma, believe me, that at the beginning some of us really tried.'

She didn't believe him at all. What a crocodile.

By now dessert was being served and with great relief, Emma embraced the etiquette that permitted her to turn to the serious, bespectacled botanist from Berwick-on-Tweed. For the remainder of dinner she encouraged him, while grateful for such rare interest, he talked non-stop about the process by which sand dunes could be reclaimed from the sea.

In the Combination Room others captured Emma for coffee. But afterwards her quarry ambled over and again took her hand.

'A drink with me?' he enquired, with more hope than expectation in his voice.

'I'm afraid not,' said Emma with as much regret as she could truthfully muster, which wasn't much. 'The Master has invited me...'

RotTEN AT THE CoRE

'Emma. You have taken grave advantage of me. I am surprised; indeed, I am hurt.'

'The Master's wife will be there,' said Emma, with a twinge of guilt that, thankfully, didn't last.

'Wives are never an impediment. *Tant pis.* Enjoy Brussels and don't forget what I have told you. By the way, there are three more things I want to mention. DG VI has a most unsavoury reputation and in asking you to do this report your Commissioner will be concealing a hidden agenda. I would be fascinated to know what it is. Secondly, in your excursions through DG VI you may have come across Céline Bardot. Her knowledge of the Commission is unrivalled. She'll know all about hidden agendas.'

Well, I never, thought Emma. If I find out, I'll take care not to tell you.

'Thirdly, be exceedingly careful...'

'Why?'

'Because otherwise you'll get very fat.'

And once again he bent to kiss her, but this time she turned in the other direction and now her right cheek received the wet embrace.

CHAPTER SIX

The Cucumber Directive

---

*A cucumber should be well sliced, and dressed with pepper and vinegar,
and then thrown out, as good for nothing.*

Samuel Johnson: 5th October, in *Life of Johnson* vol v

When, three weeks later, Emma was driving to Brussels,
Partridge's injunctions were hardly ringing in her ears. She
had other things to worry about. Just beyond Dunkirk the
road signs defeated her, having switched out of French into
Flemish, a language she couldn't even pronounce, let alone
understand.

By the time she had bypassed Bruges she was tired.
However Brussels soon appeared, then the underpass
beneath the Basilique that dropped her into a tunnel
circling the inner city. But the signs were not always clear so
by luck rather than judgement, she popped up into daylight
at the exit to Avenue Louise.

Up the boulevard, watch for trams. Turn right, feel wheels
shudder from the broken tarmac and cobbled stones, stop at
the hotel entrance with its turquoise canopy.

'You're with us for nearly two months, Madame Austen?'
enquired the receptionist.

'Yes,' said Emma.

'May I suggest you put your car in our garage
immediately? It is unwise to leave it on the street.'

'Why? Do they get stolen?'

'Regularly. The favourites belong to Commission officials.'

'They're probably the most luxurious – or is it the diplomatic number plates that provide the temptation?'

'Both, madame – and some of the chauffeurs are also attractive.'

Leaving her bags in the lobby she drove underground, but after ten minutes' struggling in a twenty-three-point turn decided the term 'dangerous' was relative. The cars were jammed in tightly, on two layers as in a haulage truck. Having finally parked on a top deck, she teetered back down the metal slope and decided that from now on it was mostly going to be taxis.

At the desk she was handed a telephone message.

'Weekends in Brussels are dreary affairs. Come and have dinner tonight. Sybilla Høgstrøm.' An address in Avenue Fond'roy followed.

Well, that's nice of her, thought Emma, as she unpacked. She hadn't really seen anything of Sybilla on her first visit, but merely registered the friendly presence of an elegant person.

She was somewhat surprised when the taxi deposited her in an obviously wealthy area of the city – a curved avenue of mature trees and solidly-built houses.

Sybilla opened the door. Dressed in finely tailored trousers, blue silk shirt, with collar carried high on the neck, she looked cool and relaxed.

'You must be exhausted,' and putting her hand on Emma's shoulder, drew her into the hall.

'Not as much as I expected. I broke the journey with friends on Romney Marsh.'

'That's good. But welcome to Brussels. Everyone is going to say that to you in the next few days.' Sybilla leant forward and kissed Emma first on her right cheek, then her left. Her hair smelt of expensive perfume. 'What you need right now is a large drink.'

She led the way into a sitting-room that ran across the house from front to back. French windows gave on to a patio and a manicured lawn with tidy flower-beds.

'Put your feet up and relax. I'll be back in a minute.' This was more of a command than an invitation, but, Emma sensed, this was Sybilla's personality – functional and very assured.

She glanced around. Contemporary Danish furniture, a round walnut table in the bay window, heavy Swedish crystal vases, a vast Persian carpet on the floor and flowers everywhere. Clearly Sybilla was wealthy enough to go through life taking a large number of things for granted.

She returned with a bottle in a cooler and two glasses. The white wine was spicy and delicious. Emma drank gratefully, then became inquisitive.

'How long have you been in the Commission?'

'Over four years now, but you must understand I didn't arrive by the orthodox route.' The implication of privileged access was unmistakable.

'And that is...?'

'You take a series of examinations – and you must never, never cheat.'

Emma returned Sybilla's mischievous look with a knowing smile. Who could forget the examination scandal of 1998 when thousands of aspiring bureaucrats were caught in wholescale cheating?

'Then you go in at a low level and work your way up. But the Danish Ambassador was a friend of my father's. So I had a job in our Mission and then the Danish government paid for me to join the *cabinet* of the last Commissioner. People are always happy to have a highly placed Dane in Agriculture. Reform of the CAP is a sensitive issue and since they think we're all farmers, they believe we'll be completely co-operative!'

'...and preserve the status quo?'

'Precisely.' Again she gave Emma her mischievous look. 'And their trust is not misplaced. You must never forget our Cucumber Directive.'

'Your what?'

'Denmark's finest hour. A widely acknowledged "paradigm of Eurocracy" that confirmed our bureaucratic reliability! Two thousand brilliant words specifying the correct length, circumference, curvature and crookedness of every cucumber for sale in the Community. Who could ever doubt us after that?'

'I love it,' said Emma. 'Do your parents still live in Denmark?'

'No, alas; they're both dead. We had problems with the family business. The stress killed my father and his death broke my mother's heart. So I was glad to be in another country. Let's eat.'

She led the way across the hall to a large dining-room and a round table covered with a blue and white batik cloth where she proceeded to serve an exquisite meal. A salad of mixed green leaves and toasted goat's cheese, with walnut oil dressing, was followed by fish Emma didn't recognise – poached in a light sauce, served with new potatoes and a dry Pouilly Fumé. Emma was ravenous and cleared her plate.

'You're a wonderful guest. It's most gratifying.'

'You are a wonderful cook. I haven't had a meal like this for a long time.'

'Excuse me while I check the soufflé!'

Emma sat back, satisfied but not sated, feeling that if pressed she could probably force down a mouthful of soufflé. Fatigue was fading for the wine had sedated her nicely. She heard the chink of utensils, glasses being set down, a phone ringing and then Sybilla's voice: 'It's not really difficult, Antoine. Try keeping the ingredients at room temperature.'

'You enjoy cooking?' queried Emma, as she took her first spoonful of passion fruit soufflé.

'I love it,' said Sybilla. 'I find it very relaxing. Coffee...?'

She was watching Emma intently as she spoke but Emma was not totally at ease, though not certain why. Tired probably: it had been a very long day.

'...and liqueur? Come and see the collection – one of my small vanities. I only have unusual ones.'

Emma read the labels of the front three bottles in the antique cupboard – *Noix de Poissy, Myrto, Frangelica* – and decided that in Sybilla's world popular liqueurs would be vulgar ones.

'I was given the *Frangelica* during our recent mission to Piedmont. It's absolutely authentic. Would you care to try?'

'No, thank you.' And she gently stepped back.

Sybilla sensed Emma's discomfort. 'I'll call a taxi. If there's anything I can do to help while you're here, all you have to do is ask.'

First thing Monday morning it was back to Breydel. Arthos, having established her in a small office on the seventh floor adjacent to the Commissioner's conference room, thoughtfully pointed out the location of supplies and the ladies' loos.

Then they walked through the very heart of Euroland, along the Rue de la Loi – the dreariest of streets down which traffic relentlessly poured. Every day Emma would travel the pounding thoroughfare – a narrow artery cutting through uninspiring buildings, all sliced off at a uniform height one determined no doubt, she thought irreverently, by a European directive.

Finally, in Rue Joseph, they came to DG VI. It was another beige office block. Outside, the concrete was relieved by a few trees. Inside, the landmarks along the narrow corridors were equally few and unmemorable, so Emma took care to memorise the route, otherwise she'd be lost. The place was a rabbit warren, packed with scurrying, serious people who looked as uniform as the buildings.

Eventually she found some light relief. Every day she met the same two Italians in the canteen. Dressed in neat grey suits, blue shirts, blue ties, they carried identical Burberry mackintoshes over their arms. They were the epitome of acceptable Commission staff members, and differed only because one favoured darker shades – his suit a darker grey, his shirt a darker blue, his tie a darker indigo. Charming and amusing, their laughter was infectious though they didn't belong in the building at all, but another Directorate up the road.

So one day Emma asked why they came to DG VI so regularly.

'Because the food here is best.'

'Well, so it should be in Agriculture.'

'That is so. Please join us for coffee, Madame,' and produced their business cards.

Aware of current gossip, Emma asked: 'So Senor Prodi is to be the next President of the Commission?'

'Yes,' the twins chorused, 'and this will be very good for Italy.'

'Why?'

'Because we will get all the money.'

There was a refreshing directness about this pair, Emma decided. She didn't think they were joking.

Of Marais' *cabinet* she saw Arthos and Céline most. Arthos was her sounding-board; Céline, the reluctant provider. Papers, files, memoranda, had to be extracted with the sweetest of polite persuasion, to be released with a deep sigh and 'You must appreciate this is most unusual.'

'But *is* it all that unusual?' she asked Ned one evening, during her regular phone calls to Cambridge.

'The extent of the access you're getting certainly is. Have you discovered Marais' hidden agenda yet?'

'Not yet...but then I'm not really looking.'

'So how's the work?'

'I tell you one thing. If I hadn't been brought in by someone at the top, the job would be impossible. And, by the way, Ned, I could be seduced by these people. They are so earnest. But where are the Belgians? This is their capital after all.'

Ned chuckled, 'They are hard to find and if you do, they're hard to know.'

Next day she asked Arthos the same question. They were in her office trying to confirm the chronology of certain key decisions in the BSE saga. Taken aback by her abrupt change of subject, he stammered, 'Well, I don't really know, Madame Austen. They are somewhat ambivalent about us so probably they're hiding.'

'I'm not surprised,' said Emma, promptly. 'You take the plum jobs in the city; you pay no taxes; you are the reason why rents have risen, and you have diplomatic immunity.'

Arthos was not about to take this lying down. 'But we are conservatives, which they like; we cause no trouble, and we have put Brussels on the map!'

'*Touché.*'

'However, I understand that real Belgians are easy to identify because they don't make jokes. So how would you say "yes" in Flemish, Madame Austen?'

'I can't say anything in Flemish.'

'Well, it's *non, peut-être.*'

'That's not a Belgian characteristic,' she objected. 'It's a Commission one.'

'*Touché,*' replied Arthos, grinning.

44

She didn't see Marais for a couple of weeks. Arthos told her that his earlier mission to Piedmont had been satisfactory, though he'd been indisposed during the trip and the Musketeers had been concerned. But then one day, unannounced, he dropped into her office.

'I am so glad to see you again, Madame Austen. Is everything going well? My staff are being helpful, I trust?'

The hidden steel in his voice said 'if they're not they soon will be.'

Emma was delighted to see him again. Her eyes sparkled and Marais was enchanted.

'I can see that you're perfectly happy,' he said without giving her a chance to reply.

'Thank you. I really am.'

Yet when he had left, after saying they must lunch together one day, she was reminded of that hidden agenda and as the days went by the thought constantly nagged at her. For one by one every member of the *cabinet* had made some excuse to drop into her office and enquire, subtly or not so subtly, how she was getting on.

The *chef* came first, with a timid knock at her door.

'Madame Austen, I am most happy to see you.' Felice Fede shot his cuffs. 'I trust Arthos is being helpful.' He hesitated, then shot them again. 'However, there is one matter you might like to know.'

Emma's mind raced. What could this be? The files had all been stolen; the minutes of meetings were written by ghost-writers; a virus had infected the computers and bliss, oh bliss, all decisions erased. But what Fede said next was utterly surprising.

'Madame Austen.' This time he adjusted his tie; she'd never seen that before. 'You will, I think, appreciate the fact that the Commission never reports to national governments the fees or expenses paid to any visiting consultants.'

Well I'm damned, thought Emma. He's telling me I can avoid British income tax. Laughing inside she tried to appear solemn. 'How very interesting,' she finally observed, knowing it was more than the reputation of Components was worth – let alone her own – if she acted on the information.

But still Fede didn't leave.

'Madame Austen, you will know that current issues are exceedingly sensitive and it is vital our decisions do not go beyond the confines of this Directorate. So before submitting your report to Commissioner Marais, it might be wise to discuss your conclusions with those of us who have been in the Commission for many years, who are totally familiar with all possible implications. I am, of course, speaking in my capacity as *chef de cabinet.*'

The words were tortuous, but only an idiot could fail to get the point.

Fede waited expectantly.

I'm damned if I'll discuss anything, thought Emma, so merely inclined her head. Fede waited, and so too, did she.

Finally she brought the meeting to a close with the sweetest smile she could muster. 'Thank you so much for coming to see me.'

Dashöfer tried next and this Emma hadn't expected. He stopped her in the corridor.

'Madame Austen.' The beard bristled through his smile and he spoke rapidly, 'I want you, please, to understand that though we Germans felt obliged to maintain the beef ban, the lifting of which we feel was premature and ill-advised, there is nothing personal in this. Indeed, if you turn up anything of importance in your research that you feel might influence our attitudes please let me know and I will see that word gets to my national authorities.'

Tortuous again, but the meaning crystal-clear. Emma struggled to control her laughter. He's a perfect example of

46

a malevolent neutral, and I'm damned if I'll tell him anything, either.

Though Céline Bardot never asked direct questions, her fussy agitation made it clear that she ached to know what Emma was likely to conclude. As she counted the files out and counted them back in, she would throw out phrases of striking originality such as 'there is so much room for misunderstanding', or parrot Fede, 'it is vital that sensitive matters never get into the public domain'. But while dying to ask for an example of a truly sensitive matter that should under no circumstances ever appear in the public domain, Emma felt Olympian detachment should remain her hallmark.

Sybilla Høgstrøm's approach was so indirect that at first Emma wondered if one had been made. Then when she realised it had, she became angry. She had been invited to dinner in the Avenue Fond'roy along with six other guests – three businessmen, a well-known BBC correspondent, the German Ambassador to Brussels and the Commissioner. Marais, charming and amusing, was on her left at the circular table, the Ambassador on her right, next to Sybilla.

When making the introductions, Sybilla had mentioned that Emma was researching the beef crisis and during dinner the Ambassador began to probe. Like Willi Dashöfer, he began with a qualifying preamble – about how this was not personal, how his country's refusal to accept British beef must not be construed as anything but a decision taken on behalf of consumer safety...

Emma was needled, 'and not on behalf of German farmers?'

'Well, of course there may be an element of this – not unnaturally so. But no, not really. All our decisions are taken exclusively on scientific grounds. I trust and expect that nothing in your research is revealing otherwise?' He turned to include Sybilla in the question and it was then that Emma suspected this was planned.

She was really indignant. This was hardly the time or place. So with a polite excuse she turned back to Marais, looked at him intently and for some unfathomable reason thought: I bet he was a wonderful father. In the years since her own father had abandoned his family, Emma had thought about him often, always with sorrow that he had played so small a part in her life.

'Did you enjoy your trip to Italy, Commissioner?' she now enquired.

'Well, yes and no. I was unwell for a couple of days. Something I ate, I think. But I love Piedmont. As a family we used to go there every summer.'

He looked sad.

'You have two children, I believe.'

'Yes. My son, Thierry, has taken over the family firm, to my great delight. But my daughter, Josephine, married an American and lives in California. My wife was American.'

Emma noticed the past tense.

'She died nine months ago. And Thierry's fiancée was killed in that Swissair crash over Newfoundland.'

Oh, my God, thought Emma, no wonder he looks sad. They've had a terrible time.

During coffee she watched the group as Sybilla began offering the liqueurs from Poissy and Piedmont along with chocolate hazelnut truffles. Most refused politely, save Marais who refused very abruptly. Sybilla, obviously taken aback by his abruptness, recovered quickly, then looked at him with an unmistakable air of possession.

Emma caught the look and was disconcerted. God Almighty, she thought, they're lovers. Why do I mind? Frenchmen always took lovers, so she understood! Marais was lonely – still mourning the loss of his wife. What could be more natural?

But she felt desolate. She might be professionally successful, but something was missing. She couldn't deceive herself forever.

The Three Musketeers didn't delve at all, however. Emma lunched with them regularly, enjoying their company and their spats, one of which confirmed her suspicion that Arthos was set apart. He had been expounding some gem of political wisdom when another Musketeer interrupted.

'Madame Austen, don't ever believe a word Arthos says. He's totally unreliable.'

'Me?' queried Arthos, in noisy horror, 'Me? Unreliable. *Incroyable*. In fact: *au contraire*. It's you damned *énarques* who think you know everything and it's high time you learnt, you don't.'

I was right, thought Emma. He didn't go to the *Ecole Nationale d'Administration*. But is he insecure about his future, or only that the others imply he's bound to be? She moved to deflect their thrusts.

'You know, I'm in Breydel almost every day but I've hardly seen the other Commissioners. Are there any? Do they get in too early for me, or something?'

They roared with laughter.

'If you don't see them,' one volunteered, 'it's because they're not there. Not many put in a full working day. Ours is an exception. Some only come in two days a week. Others regularly miss the weekly meeting. There's a rumour that in future, Prodi will insist they bring a letter of excuse from their parents if they are absent!'

'I just don't believe it. What are they doing all the time?' Emma, who had visions of Ministers of the Crown working regular exhausting hours and a full working week, was astonished.

'Do you want the charitable answer or the uncharitable one?' grinned Arthos.

'Both.'

'The charitable one says that they've been told not to stay in their ivory towers, so they go on highly enjoyable missions. The mildly uncharitable – but truthful – one is that they're at home; the grossly uncharitable, also truthful is that they're playing golf. Study the Friday press releases. These tell you what the Commissioners will be doing over the weekend. You will often find that the locations of their activities can be exactly correlated with a nearby golf course.'

'You've got to be joking,' insisted Emma.

'We're not.'

The days passed rapidly. As she watched the expansion of her report so too did she watch her waistline. She had several dangerously close encounters – with *sausage stoemp* – the Belgian version of sausage and mash, with thirty-five ways of cooking *moules* and twenty-five varieties of beer. Soon she limited herself to one course at any meal, otherwise she would have had to buy an entirely fresh wardrobe – and that her bank balance could not accommodate, even if she failed to declare her fees to the taxman!

In her free time, she had tried to find the real Belgians and the real Brussels. She even followed Joseph Conrad to the narrow Rue Bréderode. But, as he wrote in *Heart of Darkness*, all remained hidden – 'in deep shadows and dead silences'. Still, once off the ghastly Rue de la Loi, Euroland was lively enough. Travel agencies stood cheek by jowl with ethnic restaurants of every kind; the Danish design gallery was in spitting distance of the Kitty O'Shea pub, and even just a few steps away from boring DG VI, she could sit in the charming garden of the Square Marie-Louise and enjoy the fountain.

As for the work, she knew that she had a good grasp of the overall picture, though nothing she'd discovered undermined Partridge's insistence that politics and national interests mostly drove the decisions. But soon she was so comfortable in her relationships with the *cabinet* that she quickly forgot both their probing and Marais' hidden agenda. Then suddenly, three different sets of events jolted her out of complacency and she knew she had indeed been seduced by these earnest people and was never again able to regard any of them in the same light.

CHAPTER SEVEN

Growing Old in Fraud

To mischief trained, e'en from his mother's womb,
Grown old in fraud, tho' yet in manhood's bloom.
Adopting arts, by which gay villains rise,
And reach the heights, which honest men despise.

Charles Churchill: *The Times*

Emma kept flexible office hours so often went into Breydel as the bureaucrats were drifting out. Yet if her schedule was improvised, her methods never were. Computer files and papers were meticulously ordered, written reports carefully planned.

So, when one day her controlled clutter appeared disturbed she spotted this at once. It was probably the janitors she guessed and promptly dismissed the thought. Two days later her papers were again obviously disturbed, but since they contained nothing sensitive – Felice Fede's views notwithstanding – she was still not concerned, though she now locked everything away in the filing cabinet.

But soon she was troubled. The next morning she read reports, then interviewed people all afternoon. So when, in the evening, she opened up her computer it was for the first time that day. Bringing up the documents menu, she spotted a file at the top that had no business there. Recently opened files always appeared above ones opened earlier, but this one had not been used for weeks.

She frowned at her stupidity. She must have inadvertently opened the file, then immediately closed it. Yet since she was currently battling with the third section of her report, she had no reason to return to earlier sections that had been safely tucked away weeks before. So why was that file up there?

Another week passed uneventfully. Then, again one evening, she found her current working file had disappeared not only from the screen but from the hard disk too. Now she really was puzzled: her computer skills were good; she made copies on the hard disk automatically; she would not – could not – have erased working material without remembering. Was someone hacking into her files? Cursing softly, she now copied everything remaining on to clean floppy disks to take home, and with increasing fury, spent the next three hours reconstructing the missing conclusions of her third section. Now she really was worried.

Then, four days later her unease intensified for on accessing the system she saw a message: Take care to reach the right conclusions.

She felt a frisson of anxiety. Why did her conclusions matter so much? To whom did they matter? Even though Quatraro, poor devil, had long since gone – the puzzle of his death still unresolved – were criminal conspiracies still pervasive within the deep shadows of DG VI? Should she tell anyone? At that moment there was a tap at the door and Arthos entered.

She had never been more pleased to see his cheery face. By now obviously devoted to her, he was being teased unmercifully by the other Musketeers.

'Madame Austen,' he said, then stopped. 'Madame Austen, are you all right? You look pale. You work too hard, you know.'

'I think that must be it,' she replied, wondering whether to quiz him about computer break-ins. But hackers were everywhere and if they broke into the Pentagon's computers, then why not the Commission's? So she said nothing.

Yet within another week she believed she knew who was behind the problem. By now she could find her way around Breydel blindfolded and it was only because she was preoccupied – thinking with pleasant anticipation of Cambridge, home and friends – that one evening she walked straight passed her office door and into the conference room. A thoroughly startled Céline Bardot turned around and quickly put the phone down.

'Emma. What on earth are you doing here?'

'Working late. And so are you, I see.'

Céline did not reply. Something is wrong, thought Emma. Céline was looking disconcerted; her hands held still at her side. I surprised her. Has she been rifling my desk? Suddenly Céline gestured to the pile of papers.

'I'm checking the files. The Commissioner takes them home. He works all the time, you understand. But I have to be sure that none are missing.'

She gathered the pile into her arms.

'See you tomorrow,' she said cheerfully and left.

Then the phone rang. Emma was puzzled: it must be for Céline? But who knows she's here? She lifted the receiver and heard a man's voice.

'Well, do you have the information?'

Her curiosity struggled with bafflement but irreverence came to predominate and she wanted to reply, 'Yes, but I don't feel like giving it to you.' However, she just said: 'This is Emma Austen,' and the line went dead.

Back in her own room she began working. Ten minutes later the same phone rang again, so persistently that finally Emma could bear it no longer. As she moved next door she said to herself, I know what a proper receptionist would say: 'This is the European Commission. Emma Austen speaking. How may I help you?' Perhaps it would be Henry Kissinger. How delighted he would be to talk to someone in Europe!

The same voice spoke again.

'You've had sufficient time.'

'Who's that speaking, please?'

This time the sound of an expletive was unmistakable, as the phone was slammed down. No, definitely not Henry Kissinger.

Across the hall the same farce was being played out. Charles Marais was signing some letters since he would not be in the next day. He had firmly told his secretary to go home and equally had made it clear to Céline Bardot – who was nervously fussing around with questions about the files – that she should leave him. His voice was uncharacteristically abrupt so she backed out, apologising. Then the phone in his secretary's office began ringing, so incessantly that he went over and picked up the receiver. He heard a man's voice, but the words sounded garbled.

Five minutes later, another phone rang in another office – and rang and rang. With a furious 'Damn', he flung his pen down, crossed over the corridor into an adjacent room and picked up the receiver.

'Charles Marais,' he said. This time he distinctly heard the word, '*Merde*'.

What the hell is going on, he wondered and with a faint hope that someone might be around who could sort it all out, he went towards the conference room where yet another phone was ringing, and met Emma coming out.

This is just like a stage farce, she thought. Exit *cabinet* member, upper stage right; enter consultant, lower stage left. Principal stands still, stage centre.

'Madame Austen, you're working very late. But you do, I've noticed.'

He smiled engagingly, but Emma thought he looked thoroughly preoccupied and though listening with her full attention, she felt that familiar, but now thoroughly unwelcome thought making its way to the surface. During her final two weeks of work she had ruthlessly suppressed all thoughts of hidden agendas. Then she realised Marais was asking her a question and snapped out of her reverie.

'...I trust Arthos has already mentioned this. I would like to take you out to dinner the evening before our final meeting. Is this convenient?'

'Arthos did mention it. Thank you. I would be delighted.'

Marais smiled. 'The meeting will not be easy, so we might as well enjoy life while we can. Good night.'

Returning to her office Emma closed down her computer. She needed to think. Though everyone suspected fraudulent activities were pervasive in and around the Commission, she had never expected these to impact on her work. She reviewed some possible explanations of her recent problems. Her own incompetence? She didn't believe so. Hackers with a juvenile sense of humour? Possibly. She really must ask Arthos if they had disruptive cuckoos in their computer nests. Perhaps it was direct interference by people worried about her conclusions. Céline would best fit that description. For she was a guardian of the flame, her career totally devoted to the Commission. Fiercely protective of the College's image, she was too fearful to allow the bracing winds of democratic involvement – let alone exposure – to blow into the bureaucratic corridors.

People like Céline would always sweep disturbing facts under the carpet, expel whistle-blowers from office – and do so in the belief that they were acting in everyone else's best interest. This would be quite enough to explain her actions, fraud need play no part.

But then, though it began totally innocuously, a third event showed that fraud did play a part. One morning Arthos popped his head round her door.

'Ever been to the noon press conference? Would you like to? We're fielding questions today.'

Emma, cross-eyed with concentration, was glad of any excuse to get up from her desk and leave the computer screen.

'Ah, but it's not that easy. To gain admittance you must get past the lady who guards the gates. She's been in charge of the press for years and the entire corps of journalists is terrified of her.'

Promptly at 11.45 a.m., Arthos took Emma to reception and introduced her to an Italian fireball, a minute lady, sparking with professional energy that even the thickest of spectacle lenses could not hide.

'You may attend just this once, Madame Austen. But under no circumstances are you to ask any questions.'

Perish the thought, said Emma to herself, trying to appear suitably terrified. So she said very meekly, 'I quite understand.'

'Then you may go in.' She spoke to the security guard, then turned back to a pernickety old lady who had somehow got into Breydel and was demanding a tour of the Commission's headquarters, then and there. She was within her rights, she insisted: she was a European taxpayer.

'But we only have tours on one day a year.'

'Why only one day a year?' The inquisitor – who was English – was vastly irritated.

The gatekeeper didn't hesitate a moment: 'This is not Windsor Castle, Madame,' she said crushingly.

Couldn't have done better myself, thought Emma admiringly, as she walked down the stairs to the basement and entered another world. The low ceilinged room was entirely given over to the press. A television monitor flashed information; tables held reports in every conceivable language; slotted wooden compartments, prepared press releases and statements. From the wall photograph portraits stared down – Commission press spokesmen going back to 1958. Coffee tables offered refreshments and low armchairs, rest for weary limbs. Booths with telephones along one wall provided for rapid transmission of copy. Above all was something she had never met in any other Commission building – a thick pall of tobacco smoke.

She grabbed a cup and stood to one side of the chattering journalists, feeling a real intruder. Then a hand came down so firmly on her shoulder that she spilled her coffee and swore. From behind two arms enveloped her in an enormous bear-hug, and a voice declared with unmistakable Scottish authority, 'Emma, you don't belong here. I shall arrange to have you thrown out.'

Turning she saw a friend from university days, Hamish Mannock – thirty-five-ish, a considerable reporter – large in build and reputation. Unlike the formally attired people she met every day, he was dressed in jeans and a bright red shirt.

'Hamish, dear Hamish,' she said, 'I knew you were in Brussels, but didn't know how to get hold of you. Who are you working for now?'

'I'm freelance. But I know who you're working for.' He grinned.

'You do? How did you find out?'

'Not by attending the press conference, that's for sure!'

She wouldn't get anything else out of him.

'You'll come in with me,' said Hamish, 'and that way you'll look less of an imposter.'

At five minutes to twelve, he steered her into a room that reminded Emma of a classy movie theatre, except that instead of a screen there was a rectangular table with microphones on the stage. She found the backcloth unbelievable: a curved panorama in the ubiquitous

58

European Union blue, decorated with just four large, five-pointed gold stars. Why not the Union fifteen? At any moment Emma expected a flash of lightning and the President would appear, open his briefcase to show it was empty, then, hey presto, a BSE-free cow would materialise.

As they waited for the show to start, Emma flopped back in an exceedingly comfortable seat and quizzed Hamish.

'Well, first of all,' said Hamish, 'forget Jeremy Paxman. Actually, it's surprising how polite we are considering how frustrated we are. It's like punching cotton wool. You make no bloody impression at all – one of the most maddening jobs I've ever had. Everything is provided in abundance, except information. You'll see.'

'Are you especially polite if the President comes?'

'Especially polite, but he rarely comes. The only time Santer was given a rough ride was during the latest Parliamentary flare-up. Emma: you must remember – everything in Brussels takes place as a result of deliberate calculation. So if you're a high Commission official you ask: "what would you gain by subjecting yourself to these barbaric journalists?" Humiliation. Exposure. Equally, you will also consider – oh, so carefully – how your answers will be regarded by the French or Germans, since they drive the train. Best avoid the experience if you can.'

On the dot of noon the lights went down and the actors appeared. One after another, various officials came to the table, read the printed queries and prepared answers. Then the journalists tried to question them.

Emma was vastly amused. Everything Hamish said was true. When, after twenty minutes, he sighed deeply 'I've just about had enough,' she rose thankfully. She heard the soothing mantra too many times: 'the situation is very complicated and many proposals need to be considered.' In the press room he said, 'I'm going to take you to lunch. But give me fifteen minutes while I talk to people. I learn much more this way.'

Hamish retrieved her from the main lobby and once out of Breydel steered her left to Euroland's epicentre, the Place Schumann, and on into Rue Franklin. Emma was glad of the exercise: it was not too bad a day for Brussels. The grey clouds were broken up by small patches of blue and it wasn't raining and it wasn't cold.

Hamish led the way through a small entrance passage and across a courtyard, into L'Atelier. Lunch was popular; the restaurant crowded. The waiters, smartly dressed in black trousers and white shirts rushed around in controlled mayhem and didn't drop a thing.

Emma chose beef carpaccio and salad; Hamish ordered mussels and a bottle of red wine.

'Are you enjoying things?' he asked, as they clinked glasses.

'This or Brussels?'

'Both.'

'Well, schizophrenia has finally arrived,' replied Emma.

'We all succumb but remember, schizophrenia is better than war.'

'Is war likely?'

'Well, you think not, and then before you know where you are Bosnia arrives, followed by Kosovo.'

'Hamish, tell me: does Commissioner Marais have a hidden agenda? If you know what I'm doing you should know that, too.'

'Of course he does: they all do. But the real question is does his *cabinet*, especially his *chef*, know what it is?'

'Why?'

'Because the *chefs* control things. They meet every Monday morning without fail. It's supposed to be for co-ordination and harmony – to use their jargon. But what they really do is to find out what other Directorates are plotting and how the votes are stacking up for their own proposals. They can really gang up, decide agendas, move matters in any direction they choose. So if you have a weak Commissioner with a strong *chef*, then all sorts of subversions...' he stammered, '...start up.'

Emma giggled, 'You nearly said perversions, didn't you? How Freudian.'

Hamish hastily drank some water.

'Slip of the tongue. A mussel went down the wrong way.'

'Liar.'

'There's some deeply dishonourable people around. But we all know that your man controls his *cabinet*.'

'How did he get the job?'

'Most unexpectedly. You have to remember Emma, bringing a Frenchman in as Commissioner of Agriculture was highly unusual. There was a bitter clash about Marais' appointment. Yet everyone finally agreed, because the CAP *has* to be reformed – though the way things are going it never will be – and French farmers needed to be reassured. Marais was considered the perfect instrument.'

'Hmm,' said Emma thoughtfully, chewing her beef. 'I think they got more than they bargained for.'

'We know they did. He's totally his own man and I worry a bit about that.'

'Why?'

Hamish merely shook his head, disarmingly, but Emma wasn't having it.

'I bet fraud and the Quatraro affair are all part of his hidden agenda,' Emma continued, equally disarmingly.

'Where the hell did you learn about Quatraro? There's a clamp-down on that affair.'

'I asked a question at the press conference. Seriously, is it relevant?'

'It has to be.'

'So should I enquire further?'

Hamish shook his head again.

'Emma, I know you. You're far too curious for your own good. I warn you – and I'm deadly serious. It can be very dangerous to be interested in fraud in Brussels. There's a villa not far away, known to be owned by a mafia chief, where Commission officials are regularly entertained. But don't ask me for the address because I won't reveal it. I don't want to see you with concrete around your ankles.'

'Hamish, I wasn't interested in this at all at the start. Not my job. But odd things have been happening. My desk's been rifled and some files have disappeared.'

Still Hamish hesitated. He really loved her: she was courageous, intelligent and questioning and would have made a damn fine journalist. Then he compromised.

'I'm going out to UCLAF this afternoon.'

'UCLAF?'

'The Unit for the Co-ordination of Fraud Prevention. Got to see one of my sources. He'll know something. Want to come along?' He called for the bill.

CHAPTER EIGHT

Riding the Carousel

What's lost up on the roundabouts, we pulls upon the swings!

PR Chambers: *Green Days and Blue Days: Roundabouts and Swings*

The ride out to the Avenue de Beaulieu took twenty minutes. As they drove, the streets became greener, Hamish's mood lighter.

'I promise you a treat,' he said. 'The building's a gem.

They walked up some steps and through glass doors into a long corridor that swept the length of UCLAF's headquarters. Banks of tall trees were at the back; glass elevators were set next to metal staircases that spiralled upwards in an architectural double helix; a network of slanting metal girders supported the glass roof and everything – trees, spiral staircases, girders – was reflected in the polished floor.

At the reception desk, Hamish called the Deputy Director of Investigation, then turned to Emma.

'Okay. You can sign in. Nothing like the Scottish old boy network.'

'Do I know him?'

'You most certainly do. Remember old Euan?'

'How could I ever forget?' said Emma as she signed. Wild, Scottish, red-haired Euan had wedded formidable energy to vast physical strength, yet could dance an eightsome reel like he had wings on his feet. Ten years ago at university there had not been a trace of the Puritan. So how come he was an investigating officer in the Commission's anti-fraud squad?

Hamish read her thoughts: 'He hates injustice. We can go up.'

Security here was far more relaxed. There was no sign of the sniper rifles or machine-guns, that, under pressure, a Commission spokesman admitted had been purchased for use against terrorists. No one even came down to fetch them.

But as they turned towards the elevator an entourage came sweeping out. Visiting VIPs no doubt. Then Emma saw Marais, flanked by Fede and a stunning blonde woman. Sybilla Høgstrøm, Willi Dashöfer and Arthos made up the rear. Hamish stood transfixed.

'Now what the hell is going on?' she heard him murmur.

As the procession passed, Arthos spotted Emma, smiled, gave her the broadest of winks and tossed his head happily towards Marais' beautiful escort.

They watched as courteous expressions of farewell were proffered. The Commissioner's car was already waiting; Marais and Fede were ushered in while the others took the next car.

'Now what the hell *is* going on?' repeated Hamish as they entered the elevator. 'This was deliberately staged.'

'Why are you so sure?'

'Because if Marais wanted to know anything about UCLAF he could have a quiet word with his fellow Commissioner at the Wednesday meeting.'

Euan was just as Emma remembered – thickset and sure – the quintessential security man who doesn't stand out but you know is there. He still moved lightly though.

'Nice to see you again, Emma,' he said abruptly and shook her hand.

As she had always done in the past, Emma winced, turned away, waved her hand in the air and found herself looking at a series of photographs on his wall.

'Sorry, always forget. Our rogue's gallery, don't you know – my favourite fraudsters. They concentrate the mind wonderfully.'

Emma examined them one by one. They all looked so respectable that surely none could possibly be wanted by Interpol.

Euan waved them into chairs.

'Now what can I do for you?' His Scottish brogue was stronger than Hamish's.

'Why all that ceremony out front? Deferential farewells, for God's sake, atmosphere of the gravest importance.'

'Och, Hamish, that was quite beautiful,' said Euan. 'I loved it. A public demonstration by Commissioner Marais about his concern over fraud in DG VI. He arranged to see my boss and asked probing questions about our remit – quite unnecessary, of course – because he knows it perfectly well.'

'Which is?' asked Emma.

'We investigate only one crime – fraud against the European Union budget.'

'High-risk, isn't it?'

'You've lost none of your canniness, Emma. Oh yes, it's high-risk all right. Huge sums that must be spent rapidly are handled by a small number of unelected people. But though we investigate hands in the till, ours are tied behind our backs. God bless the Schengen Convention that abolished borders for criminals but not for law enforcement agencies.'

'I had no idea,' said Emma.

'Well, I'd have thought you could've worked it out. Maybe you've lost your canniness, after all,' he teased. 'Criminal investigation is totally at the mercy of national governments.'

'Then I'm surprised you ever manage to do anything,' observed Emma.

'So are we but from time to time we do. But coming back to your Commissioner...'

'Please...'

'He also asked to see one of our Examining Magistrates – LeQuesne – privately. What went on no one knows.'

Though Emma was riveted, Hamish asked her question.

'Anything cooking for you in DG VI these days?' he asked.

'Some. What flavour will you take on the carousel?'

'On the what?' Emma had never heard the expression.

'The scams are called riding the carousel, because you collect at the start and again at the finish. You just decide what to carry. How about tomato paste as in Operation Red Gold, when the Italian authorities arrested thirty executives of the tomato processing industry. They had made tomato paste from waste tomato material deemed unfit for human consumption and destined for animal feed – a product with a zero raw material cost. But they sold it nevertheless, then claimed subsidies in excess of thirty billion lira! Bingo! Not, shall we say, a very savoury episode.

'And since you're working on beef, Emma...'

How did he know?

'...you'd probably prefer to ride with cows? A whole herd, for which subsidies have been expensively paid, appears to be living on the top floor of a high-rise office block in Rome.'

'How do you find out what's going on?'

'Not easy. Mostly information is laid. Since the people finally arrested in Operation Red Gold were well-connected industrialists, they'd probably offended someone. Didn't pay the cut, I reckon. Not an area...' he hesitated, looked at her intently, then shuffled his papers.

But Hamish pressed him. 'Current suspicions about DG VI?'

'Won't say; can't say.'

'Does Marais have a hidden agenda?'

'Of course, but he hasn't told me. You don't have to look far beyond the Court of Auditors' latest report. Five billion gone missing. I'll say only this: he's determined to find out what's going on in DG VI and make an example.'

As he spoke Emma's perceptions were being reshuffled, and suddenly she saw the *cabinet* as through a one-way mirror. Euan had said, 'What's going on', not, 'if anything's going on'. What were they all up to?

'I suppose if I asked what in particular is going on, you wouldn't tell me?'

'No more I would, for all that you're beautiful.'

'How could one set up fraud from within DG VI?'

'Dead easy if you're a high-level staff member. Do it either directly or indirectly. Give your friends privileged information about contracts coming up for tender, then help win them. Influence the decision maker – that's also dead easy if you're at a high level. The *chef* is level A2, deputies A3, long-serving people, A4.'

Emma began reciting to herself – Fede, Dashöfer, Céline, Sybilla.

'So you trot off to a subordinate and say "oh, by the way, I hear your Division's received a submission for a contract from so-and-so. They're really very good indeed. Moreover, the Commissioner wants it". The Commissioner has certainly never heard of it but they aren't going to know.'

'Suppose UCLAF found somebody in DG VI acting fraudulently? Would you tell my Commissioner?'

Euan hesitated just a little too long, then laughed.

'That's an interesting question. Only if we had reason to believe there was a serious problem. What's more likely is that someone in the Directorate would learn about our enquiries and this *might'* – and he emphasised the word, 'filter back to your Commissioner. Brussels is a leaking sieve. Many cases come to us through public denunciation, but we have to be seen to balance the rights of people who work here, against the need to uncover fraud.'

'How does public denunciation work?'

'Sometimes through a whistle-blower, as with Paul van Buitenen. But then you can expect the full force of the Commission's disapproval to descend on you – as it did on that poor bloody bastard. However, there are other ways. You can call UCLAF and your call will be treated in the strictest confidence, but...actually, it got so bad that we've set up hot lines with tape recorders – three for each member country. You would phone on the United Kingdom hot line, locals here on the Belgian one. You give your information and you're asked to leave a message saying how you can be contacted.'

'Does this work?' asked Hamish with a journalist's hungry curiosity.

'To an extent.' And Euan clammed up.

Emma, sensed it was time to leave well alone. 'I know you've some business to discuss.'

Hamish looked grateful. 'Give me half an hour, then I'll run you back to town.'

Euan added: 'There's excellent coffee downstairs and a good news stand.'

She had to wait an hour and was very reflective as she drank her coffee. So Marais' hidden agenda was combating internal fraud. But who in Marais' inner circle was caught up in the shenanigans; the *chef de cabinet*, Fede? And why did she think of him first of all? Was Céline perhaps involved?

Probably there wasn't any skulduggery at all and for one brief moment felt sorry she'd ever heard about fraud. Then she stopped herself. One should never be sorry for acquiring information: it was what one did with it that mattered – and those odd events in her office were still totally inexplicable.

That evening, in a village some ten kilometers west of Waterloo, a telephone rang in a secluded villa. After two rings the Spider picked up the receiver.

'This is Henri. Calling from Paris.'

'You have something to thay?'

'The Commissioner is becoming somewhat inquisitive.'

'How tho?'

He listened carefully for two or three minutes, then replaced the receiver.

That same evening a profoundly troubled Emma called Elmdon. Jane listened carefully, was reassuring but severe.

'Emma, I know you. Curb your curiosity and just concentrate on that report. Then come home. We love you.'

But what she hadn't told Jane was that someone else was sending her the same message – a warning on her computer screen: 'Just concentrate on beef and nothing will happen to you.'

The next day Marais had an obligatory reception at the French Embassy. Then he planned to go to Sybilla's for a quiet dinner *à deux* and sleep. He considered cancelling both events. The social minuets would tax his natural courtesy and he was tired. But he forced himself to make an effort.

The Ambassador was charming, so too was his delightful wife. Various colleagues were present including the Commissioner of UCLAF and they smiled to each other across the room. After thirty minutes of courtesies and canapés, the Commercial Attaché cornered him.

'Commissioner, may I introduce a friend who is most anxious to meet you.'

Marais glanced at the card. Dr Dieter Bengt, President of a Dresden bank.

The two men exchanged compliments, then discussed the worrying levels of unemployment in France and Germany.

Finally Bengt observed: 'Your son, Thierry, has taken over the family firm, I believe?'

'Indeed, he has,' responded Marais with the warmth his son's name always evoked. 'He's doing well.'

'So I would expect from the son of such a distinguished father. But am I right, Commissioner? At present his firm's penetration into the fast-growing markets of Eastern Europe is still small?'

Marais wasn't at all certain what was going on and hated flattery.

'You should ask Thierry himself,' he said shortly.

'I would like to have the pleasure. Perhaps you would ask him to contact me? For I feel sure there are a number of significant business opportunities we could put in his way – to everyone's advantage.'

'Such as?'

'The field is unlimited. The weakness in the Far Eastern markets triggered a surge of money into Eastern Europe. It would be a great mistake to miss such opportunities. Your Directorate has also developed many links there too, I understand. Contracts, aid programmes...'

'...that have attracted a number of questionable activities.'

'Of course.' This was said very soothingly. 'Nevertheless, these are of only minor importance compared to other prospects. They surely should not be allowed to distract us from more significant matters. These things are always a question of balance. It has been a pleasure meeting you, Commissioner.' And he moved away.

Now just what was that, wondered Marais, as he gazed at the receding back. An attempt to bribe Thierry, an attempt to buy me? Probably neither. I'm tired, I'm still deeply sad and I'm getting paranoid in my old age.

By the time he reached the Avenue Fond'roy he was drained. The welcome was soothing but later in bed his preoccupations became all too evident. Though Sybilla was infinitely understanding, nonetheless he felt humiliated, so with a courteous apology dressed and left.

He had already dismissed his chauffeur for he never expected people to wait while he conducted personal affairs. Nor did he want to add his official Mercedes to the toll of Daimlers, Jaguars, and BMWs that were the target of organised gangs in Brussels. Yet when Sybilla let him out he saw his car outside. Did his driver know him better than he knew himself?

Though misty, the night was gentle, yet still he felt suffocated. The Avenue Fond'roy was a long way from his house – way over the other side of the Bois de la Cambre, the vast wooded park at the top of the Avenue Louise. When the car reached Avenue Franklin Roosevelt, on the east side of the park, he touched his driver on the shoulder, 'I need air. Let me out and I'll walk home.'

'Certainly not, Commissioner. I cannot allow you to walk through unlit areas late at night.' And he drove on.

Marais didn't argue but waited until they had gone right round the wood and were at the top of the Chaussée de Waterloo – a main street running parallel to the park, straight downhill towards the centre of Brussels.

Now he insisted and his driver relented, letting him off at the restaurant, Terra e Mare. He crossed the road and strode on slowly down the hill, walking against the one-way flow of traffic.

At times like this he missed his native Auvergne acutely – the long, smooth sweep of the hills in Cantal, the open vistas, the vast skies, the shadows of the clouds chasing across the grass, the sudden storms. When this job was finished he would never live in a foreign country again.

He deliberately relaxed his step and suddenly the much-loved music flooded his soul. Those crystal notes, soaring upwards as larks in the summer sky. Vittoria de Los Angeles or Kiri Te Kanawa? He could never decide whose voice moved him the most and both had recorded Canteloube's, *Songs of the Auvergne.*

The accelerating car came from nowhere and came suddenly, mounting the pavement, straight at him. Though Marais had the slight hearing loss of advancing age, luckily his reflexes were those of a young man and fate also took a hand. He was near a flower shop, the porch set back from the pavement and there were three steps to the entrance. These he leapt.

With a wrench of the wheel and a screech of tyres, the car spun back onto the road, leaving him white and trembling, but no longer paranoid. The words he had heard a mere forty-eight hours ago from Magistrate LeQuesne, echoed in his ears: 'Commissioner, being interested in fraud can be very dangerous in Brussels.'

Staggering as if drunk, he tottered down past two shops and came to the Brasserie Georges at the corner of Avenue Defré and Avenue Winston Churchill. Blindly he pushed open the doors. The place was full of noise, smoke and young people who were very surprised at the intrusion. This was no place for a grandfather! He went over to the bar and said: 'Water please, and a brandy and a taxi.'

The very next day he began to assemble a dossier with files and papers from DG VI, together with his own written notes recording the episode at the French Embassy, his experiences with the car and some gossip he'd heard about Felice Fede. He kept this locked in his desk at home.

CHAPTER NINE

The Rules of the Game

The strength of science is that it has tended to attract individuals who love knowledge and the creation of it.
Just as important to the integrity of science are the unwritten rules of the game. The system of rewards and punishments make honest, vigorous, conscientious, working scholars out of people who have human tendencies of slothfulness and no more rectitude than the law requires.

Editorial in *Science*, 1963, 139, p.3561

Two weeks later, report finished and handed in, Emma took a quick break in Cambridge before returning to Brussels for dinner with the Commissioner and her final meeting.

Promptly at 7.45 p.m. Marais arrived in the hotel lobby.

'You are looking wonderful' – and kissed her hand – 'Were you glad to be home last weekend?'

'Well, actually I was rather.'

'I know the feeling.'

A fifteen-minute drive brought them to the Place Rouppe, an unpretentious square in old Brussels. The car stopped at what appeared to be a private house.

'Forgive me,' said Marais as he helped her out, 'if I am somewhat unoriginal, but I wanted to bring you here.'

Emma glanced up at the simple bay window of the most famous restaurant in Brussels, Comme Chez Soi, and took a deep breath.

'You can be as unoriginal as you like. I've been told about
this place but never imagined I'd come here. I thought you
had to book up weeks ahead.'

Marais smiled. 'You do and I did.'

How very nice of him.

As they entered a small hall a young woman, in a simple
bright red suit, came forward.

'Welcome, Commissioner,' she said.

'Thank you, Laurence.' Marais turned to face her. 'The
first thing you should know, Emma, is that Comme chez Soi
has been in Laurence's family since 1926. You're the fourth
generation, aren't you?'

'Yes. My great-grandfather was the founder and first chef.
My grandfather was the second; my father, Pierre, is the
third, and my husband is deputy chef.'

'But there is a fifth, I believe?' said Marais. 'Is the mantle
about to fall on them?'

Laurence smiled. 'Please – not just yet. Jessica is three,
and our boy, Lock, only four months.'

Marais smiled again. 'I must ensure that no EU directive
is passed to prohibit this divine monopoly!'

'We would be very grateful, Commissioner,' and took
their coats.

Marais turned to Emma again and announced firmly.

'I'm an Auvergne peasant at heart so I want to eat in the
kitchen.' And, to Emma's total astonishment, he ignored
the doorway to the right and charged through two swing
doors into the kitchen – large, bustling and pristine. The
main working areas spread out on either side; a small bay
window overlooked the elegant front dining-room. Marais
eased skilfully around older chief chefs, and younger *sous-
chefs*, silver frigidaires and gas hobs, until he reached a long
dining area – an old cellar with curved roof – in an alcove
right at the back, a table had been set for two. Emma was
enchanted.

Pierre Wynant, present chef and owner, greeted the Commissioner like an old friend. In his early fifties, his creased faced was topped by the tallest of chef's pleated hats and tailed by a dark moustache and grey beard. Twinkling eyes were hidden by large metal-framed spectacles. As he and Marais began discussing the menu, Emma turned to read some of the hundreds of signatures on the brick walls: Jack Nicklaus, Woody Allen, the four Rolling Stones. Marais was smiling.

'You'll find Ted Heath somewhere,' he volunteered.

'Ted Heath?' Emma was very surprised.

'Perhaps not. I don't think he goes in for autographs. But wait.'

He spoke to Pierre Wynant who said, 'Ah yes,' then disappeared and quickly returned with his book, *Creative Belgian Cuisine*.

'Try the preface,' invited Marais. Emma turned to page nine:

One of my greatest delights in all the time I have spent in Brussels has been to visit Comme chez Soi.

This was particularly the case when I was leading the negotiations for Britain's entry into the European Community in the 60s, and again when I was Prime Minister, culminating in my signing the Treaty of Rome at Brussels in the 70s. Indeed, so precious had Comme chez Soi become to us at that time, that we held our celebration in the restaurant, which was opened especially for us after the ceremony.

Marais chuckled. 'I bet he ate here almost every night and you British taxpayers knew nothing about this!'

'It figures,' Emma replied, recalling Ted Heath's dimensions.

'Now, champagne or the special house aperitif?'

'What's in the aperitif?'

Marais raised an interrogative eyebrow and a smiling Pierre Wynant volunteered: 'Champagne, gin, bourgogne, aligote and a double cream cassis. We call it *Apéritif Améliorant*. To make things better, is the English translation, I believe.'

Emma blenched. 'I'm not *that* unhappy. Champagne, please.'

Marais laughed. 'We'll both have champagne,' and took a decision.

'Do you know my son, Thierry?'

'You told me he was now running the family company.'

Marais raised his glass to her, then took a long thoughtful drink.

'Yes, and doing brilliantly. Has Components ever had any contact with us?'

'No, never, but you have a terrific reputation.'

'Well I think you'd like to meet him.'

Emma gave him a quizzical look tinged with laughter. He's not only planned the dinner, he's probably planned that meeting, too. But Marais was not a whit disconcerted.

'Of course! What I should have said was that I'd like you to meet Thierry. Come and have drinks tomorrow evening, after the meeting. He's here for a couple of days and then we're taking a short break in Tuscany. Shall we order?'

'I'm going to let you do that.'

'Do you mind getting messy fingers?'

'Commissioner – what a ridiculous question!'

'Charles, please,' and he beckoned the *maître d'hôtel*.

'The messy bit starts straight away with little grey shrimps,' said Marais. 'Then, since it's autumn and I am from the Auvergne, I suggest game. Partridge, I think.'

As Marais ordered a bottle of Chambertin, Emma settled back to enjoy every moment of the unaccustomed luxury –

the place, the food, the wine, the pampering and above all, the man – witty, intelligent and cosmopolitan. She caught his eyes. He had been watching, delighting in her enjoyment and raised his glass to her again.

'Comme chez Soi,' she repeated. 'Just Like Home. Oh, no. I couldn't begin to match this.'

'I agree: the name is somewhat unrealistic.'

Emma couldn't resist the next question.

'I know you're an *énarque*. Is Thierry one too?' she asked, as she tried to get her tongue round the name.

'You're doing all right,' Marais replied appreciatively. 'No, absolutely not. He flatly refused to go to our *Ecole Nationale*. We had quite an argument.'

He remembered the scene very clearly. The intense, passionate student, the amused look in his wife's eyes, her pride in the boy mixed with laughter.

'Become an *énarque* – me – turn into a very charming, very French and quite useless nerd...'

'But, Thierry...'

'...In a double-breasted suit, carrying a red box and spending other people's money...'

'Thierry...' He couldn't get a word in.

'...impeding all efforts to reform, Papa. Change. It's a new world. What France needs is not *énarques* like you, but good managers. I'm off to Harvard Business School.' – and left.

He remembered the way she took his hand, then lovingly kissed him.

'Let him go, dearest.'

She had been right – she almost always was. Oh God, how he missed her.

He pulled himself together. He must let the past go. He was dining with a delightful English colleague, who was asking him another question.

'When did your famous school start?'

'Charles de Gaulle founded it some 50 years ago. Its philosophy reflects a totally theoretical approach to government. Don't forget, we French are all sons of Descartes.'

'He had a totally theoretical approach to science, too.'

'*Bien sûr*. So he created this exclusive caste with extremely conservative ways of thinking, which penetrated into every corner of the country. Odd: though we French are fierce individualists we are surprisingly comfortable with a system where the state is very powerful.'

Fingers cleaned in water, scented with a rose petal, Emma now tackled partridge with vine leaves. The breast arrived first, in a red berry sauce she couldn't identify, along with mushrooms and potatoes done so exquisitely that even to think 'chips' would be a proletarian insult. A simple green salad with the bird's liver on the side, followed next. The legs provided the finale, served with more delicious berry sauce.

'The best cooking in Brussels?' queried Marais mischievously.

Again Emma gave him her quizzical look but said nothing.

'Now, I wonder, where else have you eaten?'

'I'm trained in law so I recognise a leading question when I hear one. You know perfectly well. You were there. Sybilla gives marvellous dinner parties, doesn't she? Such taste – exquisite cooking, beautifully prepared – but I must confess I'm puzzled by the pride she takes in that collection of liqueurs. I don't actually like them. If I remember correctly she has a couple based on nuts of all things! A strange one from Poissy and another from Piedmont, with a name like that famous Italian painter. All very confusing.'

Marais regarded her with mock severity. 'The liqueur is Frangelica, the painter Fra Angelico and please don't ever confuse him with anything. I'm totally devoted. Once I even harboured an illusion that I had found an original.'

'When was that?'

'I'll never forget,' laughed Marais. 'We were on a family holiday in Tuscany. The children had a lovely time running wild all over the countryside. Then one day I insisted on a spot of culture and took everyone down to Arezzo. Have you ever been there?'

Emma shook her head.

'Well, it's a small town full of antique shops and I went into every single one. I remember Thierry very well that day. He was grumpy beyond belief.

Anyway I was rummaging at the back of one shop and pulled out a grubby canvas. When I looked closely I believed I had a piece of a Fra Angelico painting and sent it to an art historian to be authenticated. I should have been so lucky. However, it *was* part of a copy done in the 19th century, of his *Détail du Couronnement de la Vierge*. His work became immensely popular at that time.'

'And you have a postcard on your desk, haven't you?'

'How observant you are. Dessert?'

'Please. But something light.'

'Forgive me if I just watch. I usually don't eat dessert if I can help it. However, at lunch tomorrow I'll have to. The President's Chef gets upset if you don't at least taste every dish.'

He lifted his glass again: 'Here's to you and a job very well done. I thank you so much. The way you tackled this has been most impressive and you put your finger on all the pertinent issues.'

'Well, I enjoyed doing it,' said Emma, 'though not everything I report will be welcome.'

'Don't worry. I shall deal with the fallout.'

'Do you mind if I ask you something?' Emma said slowly, wondering about his hidden agenda.

'Not at all.'

'What did you hope to achieve?'

'Use this as a case study, to help change attitudes,' he replied with deliberate vagueness.

She wanted to ask 'Whose?' but could feel his forbidding silence.

'What's triggered this?'

'Emma, you nearly said "at your great age"!' He laughed. 'I may be an *énarque*, but I find the paradoxes fascinating. Many politicians – Prodi is one – are urging ever closer political union, at a time when there are strong devolutionary movements, like those in Scotland, busy returning power where I think it properly belongs.'

'You do?' queried Emma, 'you really believe it belongs out there?'

'Surprisingly, for the old man I am, yes, I do.'

'Should you be revealing this to me?' asked Emma in mock horror.

'My dear Emma, I've been saying this for ages. Generations of my family have acquired fearless reputations for speaking their minds, then losing their lives by losing their heads. When Prime Minister Jospin recommended I become a Commissioner, the notion of public account-ability was becoming a buzz-word. I would be a good front man since I didn't have to pretend.'

'Surely they must have realised you would do more than just talk?'

'If they didn't they certainly got more than they bargained for!'

'I'm fascinated,' said Emma truthfully. 'You know, after my time here I finally understand something of the difficulties you had with us – and we with you.'

Marais rubbed at his nose a little ruefully.

'Well, at the start everyone – with the possible exception of Ted Heath – knew that the UK would have to pay through the nose. Certainly de Gaulle knew and the knowledge made him exceedingly cheerful – in fact, you could say he arranged it. Matters would never have changed if Margaret Thatcher hadn't come to power.'

'Who could ever forget her?' he went on grinning, 'the most powerful lady of all. "Thank you very much, but we'll just take a single market today," she said, as blithely as if she were shopping at Marks & Spencers. No wonder Kohl was shocked. She was shaking the pillars of the temple. Hadn't she ever heard of the Treaty of Rome?'

'But I've learnt that we do not shake alone. We and Denmark make up the Awkward Squad.'

'True – and you both have a point. Our biggest failure is the public failure.' He was speaking with quiet passion. 'Blair might well recognise this, though I mistrust his "people" prefixes. By the way, is it true that when you call Downing Street there's an answerphone that says: "Please speak after the high moral tone"?'

'Quite true.'

'But now, I'll simply have to be serious. Any problems for me tomorrow?'

Emma reflected for a moment.

'Not really. No – I'm wrong. Several, in fact. One of which is that though we can now say with certainty, yes, there is BSE, and yes there is new variant CJD, and there's an association between the two, we still haven't actually proved that humans get the disease from *eating* red meat.'

Marais sighed. 'Oh dear, oh dear. If only my problems were that simple. But I've much worse ones to contend with.'

As Emma sipped her coffee – tangy and delectable – she toyed with a card placed over the dish of chocolate-covered almonds. 'In exclusiveness with Neuhaus', it read. She chuckled. Translation was the only point where Comme Chez Soi had slipped up.

She was totally charmed by the occasion, stimulated by their talk, lulled by the controlled frenzy of the professionals in the kitchen. She heard the quiet voices and soft padding feet, the ring of metal on metal. In less than forty-eight hours this would all end – fascinating work, a touch of luxury, cosmopolitan city, interesting people. She would miss Marais above all. Yet when he next spoke her tranquillity was shattered.

'Fraud is my problem,' he said '...on a gargantuan scale and I hate it.'

In spite of the warmth of the kitchen, Emma shivered. Oh God, take care...take care, she thought, for a ghost had just walked on her grave.

CHAPTER TEN

Eating People is Wrong

I won't eat people, I won't eat people, eating people is wrong.

Michael Flanders and Donald Swann, from their review: *At a Drop of a Hat*

When Emma entered the conference room Céline Bardot was fluttering around, checking everything was in order. She was still uneasy with Emma and after a few nervous words, withdrew.

Slowly the group assembled – scientists, veterinarians and Agricultural Ministers. Right on time, Marais came in, accompanied by Arthos and Fede. He shook everyone's hands briskly, in typical French style, then motioned Emma to a seat on his right.

'Thank you for coming. You will all have received Madame Austen's report. We are at the start of a process to see how similar crises might be better handled in future. But before we begin I want to state my reasons for commissioning this work. These go back to my firm conviction that the Commission's decisions should be publicly accessible.'

Emma watched him thoughtfully. How unusual for a Commissioner – let alone an *énarque* – to talk of involving the public in decisions. Did Marais realise he was giving many hostages to fortune? She was truly puzzled, for she couldn't see the closed culture of Brussels ever changing, even though one hundred spin doctors were rumoured to be shortly arriving with Romano Prodi. But no matter how many came, the democratic fault line of governance – already of tectonic proportions – that separated continental Europe from the UK would remain as fragile as ever.

She glanced around the table. Two delegates were nodding with approval; others looked impassive; one plain bored – why did he bother to come – and those from Germany and Belgium were stony-faced.

'Madame Austen.'

Emma hesitated. She needed to martial her points clearly and carefully, for she suspected that, Marais and Arthos apart, no one had actually read a single word of her document. So one by one, she covered the questions he had initially posed, while conducting an internal dialogue at the same time.

First, had decisions always been taken on purely scientific grounds? Certainly not, and she analysed several telling examples.

Next, Marais had queried the role of the press, and in an equally careful analysis Emma was able to show that the effect of media coverage had not always been benign and there were some very unfortunate consequences. Ignoring all stony stares, she proceeded to discuss these also.

Thirdly, Marais had wanted to know how open had been the Commission's decisions. The usual mirage actually, though she stated this more diplomatically. For a start, she reviewed how public confidence had been initially shaken by the first cover-up, an episode known in Brussels as *L'Affaire de la vache folle*. A senior civil servant, Gilbert Castille, now living in the lush cattle country of Limousin, had served with Commission's Consumer Protection Agency. On 12th October 1990, following a meeting of the EU's Veterinary Committee, he drafted a memo to his superiors, describing how one Commission representative had told the Committee: 'We will not speak about BSE. This matter will not appear on any agenda... We will officially ask the UK not to publish the results of their research... On the general plan, this BSE affair must be minimised using disinformation. It is better to say that the press have a tendency to exaggerate.'

The decision to suppress such information arose from fear that consumers' confidence would be undermined. Though *Le Monde* and *Libération* actually had copies of the official minutes, the Commission – true to form – denied first the existence of the meeting, then the memo, then the minutes – which they claimed had unaccountably disappeared – and finally their own cover-up. They would have denied the existence of the Gilbert Castille too if they could, thought Emma. The European Parliamentarians were furious when it became obvious that all were alive and well.

She took great care over Marais' final question for it was highly contentious. Based on scientific statements and her reviewed evidence, she concluded that, as yet, there was no tight scientific proof that new form of CJD (nvCJD) in humans was caused by *eating* BSE infected beef.

There was a deafening silence as she finished.

'You are now invited to question Madame Austen.'

Emma waited as the shuffling of papers and clearing of throats signalled the usual dynamics. Who would jump in with what question? Marais recognised 'our colleague from Spain'.

Emma looked down the table towards the Spaniard – a head of thick wavy hair, manner, dress and English all so faultless that Emma wondered: could I imagine him dancing a passionate, wild – even abandoned – Flamenco? She decided she couldn't, no more than she could Tony Blair and he at least played the guitar. Stop stereotyping, she told herself, and as if in retribution, the Spaniard's first observations completely squashed her frivolous thoughts.

'Commissioner,' he said, 'I am truly astonished at Madame Austen's last conclusion. We have been repeatedly told of parallels between the disease *kuru* that forty years ago appeared in a tribe in New Guinea – who ate the flesh of their dead – and new variant CJD in humans now. Are all these reports wrong? Does *kuru* have no bearing on our problem?'

Emma took a deep breath. Even before the meeting began she guessed the direction the discussion would take: was the infectious agent transmitted to human beings by *eating* beef? Though she knew this was still an open question, the delegates would have to challenge any other conclusion, otherwise the whole rationale of the beef ban was totally flawed.

Since she was about to shock him, she smiled very sweetly at the Spaniard.

'There are only a few parallels and these are not very significant,' she responded. 'First, *kuru* amongst the Fore was a communal health disaster – far, far greater than anything provoked in the UK by BSE and nvCJD, now or in the future. The epidemic in the Fore women and infants was so rapid and widespread that the tribe believed they faced extinction. To have a genuinely parallel situation,' she waited, then spoke slowly, with great emphasis, 'by now, five hundred and eighty thousand people in the UK should have contracted nvCJD. So far, fourteen years since the first BSE case occurred in a British cow, we've had just fifty-two deaths.'*

'Yet a distinguished British scientist spoke of a possible plague of Biblical proportions.' Emma looked up at the speaker. German, handsome, tall.

---

* By November 2000, when the Phillips Enquiry on BSE had reported, the numbers had risen to eighty-five, and the word 'new' had been removed from variant CJD.

'I believe he will come to regret that remark,' she said evenly. 'Latest studies from the Wellcome Trust Centre, show that the initial predictions were greatly over-estimated.' She glanced at Marais, immobile, in that attitude of complete attention she knew well. But a smile was flickering in his eyes.

She turned back to the Spaniard. 'Three other features of *kuru* also set firm limits on the parallels that can be legitimately drawn. First, the epidemic occurred in a small, tightly-closed community; secondly, the people had no contact with outside influences. Finally, numbers were high enough to be epidemiologically very significant. Don't misunderstand me at all: whatever the numbers, un-necessary deaths – whether from war or *kuru* or variant CJD – are a total tragedy. However, while it's appropriate to use the word "epidemic" for *kuru* in the Fore, and BSE in cattle, I question how appropriate it is to use the word for the fifty-two cases in a UK population of fifty-eight million people.'

'You wrote that it was lucky the outbreak occurred in a small, isolated population, didn't you?' The Irish delegate. Twinkling blue eyes, thin face, pronounced laughter. I am not stereotyping now, she thought, he's a lovely leprechaun. Yet friendly though his face might be, his observations too, were designed to put her firmly on the spot.

'Yes,' Emma agreed.

'So you're implying we should be very careful in drawing such parallels. Because the simple environmental conditions of a small, isolated Stone Age tribe with *kuru*, are totally different from those of a technologically sophisticated, mobile British population who have a host of environmental factors impinging on them?'

'That's exactly what I am saying.'

'If that is the case,' the Spaniard now protested, 'Why is the parallel always made: the Fore developed a degenerative brain disease through eating meat – in their case, each other; the British victims acquired a similar disease also through eating – in this case, BSE diseased cows, who'd been fed scrapie infected sheep.'

Marais turned expectantly towards Emma. His quizzical look reflected both amusement and keen interest as to how she would respond.

'Well, that aspect is grossly misrepresented,' said Emma firmly, 'Few people had ever visited the Fore, let alone studied them – and all assumed they were traditional cannibals. But as two American anthropologists later showed, everyone got it wrong.'

'The syllogism went like this: all tribes in New Guinea are cannibals; the Fore is a tribe in New Guinea; therefore the Fore must be cannibals. Well, the second sentence apart, none of this is actually true. Yet the Australian press, who printed the first reports, found the headline irresistible – "Exotic Disease Wiping Out Cannibal Tribe" – and provided a *frisson* which has never left this story.'

Now Emma became aware of an irritated restlessness amongst the audience, like the moments before a Mexican wave surges through a crowd.

'I don't see the relevance.'

The German Agricultural Minister. He would stonewall throughout.

'Then approach this from another angle. Most scientists now believe that the source of the BSE outbreak in cattle, was not through feeding them ground-up, scrapie infected sheep, but a mutation – in a single cow alone – of a gene that codes for a brain protein. The mutation made that protein potentially lethal. Tragically, that cow was ground up and got into cattle feed. Scientists also believe that *kuru* similarly appeared in one Fore individual. Now genes can contain infectious particles – slow viruses – that during evolution have established deep genetic links with the cells they infect. Though these can remain dormant for years, later they can become active and provoke clinical symptoms of disease. Given appropriate opportunities they may even pass to other individuals.'

'All right then,' said her interlocutor, rapidly becoming her persecutor. 'What appropriate opportunity occurred in the Fore tribe? They weren't ground up.'

'Please wait. The Fore women knew very precisely when the women of an adjacent tribe, who *were* traditional cannibals, suggested they try some human flesh. They told the anthropologists that this happened shortly after "the silver bird" appeared in the sky. An aeroplane first flew over New Guinea in 1921. From that moment, when the Fore women were preparing bodies for burial, they would occasionally eat a sliver of flesh, or steam brain tissue in bamboo stems, and feed scraps to their infants, too.

'Now the agent for *kuru* had a mechanism for transmission from person to person that hadn't existed before and the disease spread rapidly. But since men took no part in funeral preparations this neatly explains why the *kuru* victims were either women or toddlers.'

'But Madame Austen, you've just given a thoroughly convincing account of how *kuru* actually *was* transmitted by eating human flesh.' The note of triumph in the voice was unmistakeable.

'You might think so, but actually I haven't. There's a crucial twist. Experience in the field must always be reinforced by experiments in the laboratory, and experimental science doesn't support that view at all. If eating human flesh was the route of transmission, we should be able to induce *kuru* in laboratory animals through feeding. But no one has ever succeeded.'

'I thought they had.'

'No,' she hit the word very firmly. 'Though the two scientists most closely involved – the Nobel Laureate, Carlton Gadjusek and his colleague, Joe Gibbs, at the

National Institute of Health – certainly tried. When they *injected* brain tissue directly into the brains of chimpanzees, the animals died from *kuru*, three years later. But when they *fed* them the tissue, nothing happened, even though massive amounts of infectious material were placed directly into the stomach through a gastric tube. And to anticipate your next question – both scientists are now convinced that the infectious agent was transmitted directly into the blood stream, either through cuts and open sores on hands, or through the mucous membranes, by the rubbing of eyes and noses.

'So I insist: we now face an identical challenge to the one faced by Gadjusek and Gibbs. If humans acquire new variant CJD through eating BSE infected meat, then we should be able to replicate this transmission in the laboratory.'

'But we have, surely?' A soft Austrian voice.

'No, we have not,' said Emma, for once welcoming a question. 'And it would appear that we're not even going to try. Joe Gibbs felt this experiment was crucial. Interviewed on British television he said, and I quote' – she turned to her notes – ' "Now we needed brain samples of British cows infected with BSE to test in chimpanzees. We were in a great position to determine whether or not the BSE material would cause disease in non-human primates. The chimps were in place, protocol and biosafety approved, money provided, but we couldn't get the brain tissue. It was never made available. I was very frustrated." '

'Why couldn't he get it?'

'One UK vet interviewed on the same programme, said that while he didn't know how much ethical issues played a part in not supplying tissue for Gibbs' purpose, they certainly would have played some. Trying to transmit the disease experimentally to chimpanzees, is not something that would ever be considered in Britain.'

A French eyebrow, attached to a scientist from the Pasteur Institute, soared skywards.

'And what do you believe?' To her astonishment the UK Agricultural Minister asked the question.

Emma had only ever seen him on television – either speaking in Parliamentary debates, or facing ferreting journalists. He had considerable dignity, she remembered, though guessed he was very cautious.

'I believe everything that can be done experimentally should be done, so there is no ambiguity at all. It's important to nail this down. We should parallel all Gadjusek's and Gibbs' *kuru* experiments. We need to see first, if BSE tissue from cattle will produce a disease in non-human primates. If it does, we need a second set of experiments – again in non-human primates – to see if the route of infection is through the stomach. Without these we will never arrive at a situation of genuine scientific proof.'

There was a rising murmur around the table from which Emma disentangled murmurs of 'I agree' from those of 'quite unnecessary'.

She decided to strike home. 'There's another puzzling factor that adds weight to this point.'

'Which is?'

'Scientists and journalists keep reporting an "unnerving" fact about nvCJD – its appearance in "unusually young" children. But how young is "unusually" young? No one under the age of fourteen has yet succumbed. But Gadjusek found significant amounts of *kuru* in children between five and ten. Now that I *do* call "unusually young". So his argument, and Joe Gibbs' too,' and now she looked directly at the German delegate, 'is this: when you consider the thousands of children in the UK who, since 1985, have eaten tons of hamburgers, if the route of infection was through eating red meat, we would expect to see nvCJD in that same, very young, age group. But we've not. Why not?'

She waited to let the fact sink in.

'One possible conclusion is that the way this issue was handled might have set up a self-fulfilling prophecy. People react to the aberrances not by asking what other reasons might explain them, but by expanding the original theory like a concertina. Yet, other possibilities should be considered. Let me explain why. First of all, we have fresh empirical evidence. Years back, there was a cluster of cases in one area of Kent; more recently, five turned up in Queniborough, a hamlet in Leicestershire; the incidence of nvCJD appears to be higher in the north of the UK; some victims were vegetarians. All these examples need explaining.

'And there are a number of alternative explanations around. Unlike with the Fore, maybe a variety of events is involved. Genetic factors clearly are; some people do appear resistant. Next, Alan Ebringer, an immunologist at King's College, suspects a runaway immune response to a common soil bacteria plays the definitive role. Then again, in 1988, Professor Richard Southwood – an independent adviser to our government – provided strong evidence that suggested a far higher risk came through hormones derived from cattle, than from meat. His advice was ignored and when senior officials were asked why, they were clearly embarrassed.'

'I see what you're getting at,' said the Austrian, prepared to meet her at least half way. 'I keep reading that though "the link between new variant CJD and eating beef is not proven, it's the most plausible, overpowering explanation." Is that good enough?'*

---

* On Thursday 20th October 2000, Professor Smith, Chairman of SEAC repeated this word on the Today programme, BBC Radio 4. 'Though we know the infectious agent for BSE and variant CJD are one and the same, we do not know how this passes to human beings. Eating infected beef is the most plausible explanation.'

'I don't think so,' said Emma, 'Though I must say that I don't think there's anything particularly sinister in this. Scientists are reluctant to give up their theories as much as the media are their *frissons*. But are you content with a situation where we don't really know how people actually contract nvCJD?'

'Yet does this really matter now?' asked the Spaniard. 'It's water under the bridge, surely. Anyway there are very few BSE infected cattle in Europe.'

'No?' came soft, unconvinced and incredulous Irish tones.

'...Abattoir hygiene in Europe is in the clear...'

'Really?' The same soft, mischievous tones again.

'So why disturb things?'

'Commissioner,' the French scientist was insistent. 'That's exactly the let-sleeping-dogs-lie attitude that got us into such trouble before. If there is any possibility that people can contract nvCJD by other routes, I damn well want to know. I remind you. I was on the Commission's Committee to review France's continuation of their ban on British beef, and though I don't like saying this, I believe my government is wrong. There are no scientific grounds for maintaining this. In any case, we're facing a significant BSE problem in France.'

'Speaking for my government,' observed the UK Minister for Agriculture, 'we most certainly are not content with a situation when we don't really know what happened. That is why we initiated our public inquiry and further experimental work,' he added, more than a trifle smugly.

Emma took good care not to look at him for fear her face would betray her. She knew the experiments he referred to were not the crucial ones Gadjusek and Gibbs wanted.

But others were on the warpath. The Belgian was conferring with the German. They looked as if they were wondering how to say 'Bullshit' diplomatically. Emma braced herself.

'Madame Austen, your stance is totally obscurantist.' The German was speaking again. 'Let me remind you: two definitive studies were recently published in *Nature* – and what scientific journal is more reputable – showing that in every single respect – symptoms, brain pathology, molecular markers – BSE in cattle was identical to nvCJD. So you get the disease from eating BSE infected meat.'

Emma hit back at once.

'This does not follow. You've ignored something very important. The Principal Investigator of the studies you've mentioned – Professor John Collinge – was interviewed on the day *Nature* published his results. I found two aspects of his interview highly significant. First, he emphasised that the time it took for the disease to show in his experimental mice was inordinate. All of five hundred days – while a normal mouse life span is far, far shorter. This showed how difficult it is for the infectious agent to cross the species barrier. More importantly, he was exceedingly careful *not* to make any connection with eating infected meat. Indeed, a few weeks later, interviewed for a BBC television series, he admitted that no such connection had been established.

'But the press made the connection all right. I heard the first reports on the BBC World Service and followed the stories throughout the day. All referred to Collinge's studies as "confirming" and "important". Fair adjectives, since the molecular identification between BSE and nvCJD was complete. But all also added that the situation was "very worrying, for eating BSE infected beef was clearly to blame." Not "probably", or "most likely", but "*was*". Not so fair.

'This was just one of many communication slips in this entire saga. You will recall other errors I found – such as when material evidence was withheld by some of your committees from other committees of yours.'

There was an uncomfortable silence. Marais glanced at his watch.

'We must break shortly and will continue this afternoon.'

But the Italian Agricultural Minister, sitting next to Fede and just as beautifully suited, now spoke.

'Commissioner, if you will permit, I have one final question. Madame Austen, your report mentioned the need to identify our real problem. Were you talking about risk?'

'Yes, I was,' said Emma, deliberately using as mild a tone as possible. 'There's a vast amount of education that needs to be done on the nature of risk, not only for society but politicians too, who show an irrational reluctance to allow the public to decide for themselves what risks they are willing to run.

'You will know where I am coming from. Since 1985, when the BSE epidemic was first identified in UK cattle, we've had fifty-two cases of variant CJD. But the number of equally fatal illnesses caused by smoking during the same fourteen years, approaches half a million. Last year alone half a million people in Europe died from tobacco related causes. Nevertheless the Community still subsidises tobacco producers to the tune of £800 million per year – to grow a crop that is a proven health risk and no one wants. Yet the European Union totally restricted the sale and export of beef that, by comparison, offers minimal risks.'

She waited for the eruption. The Spanish delegate observed this was quite uncalled for. The German protested furiously: 'Such opinions, Commissioner, were surely not part of Madame Austen's remit?' The Italian Agricultural Minister looked distinctly uncomfortable until Dr Fede touched his arm in a gesture of reassurance. Tranquillising his Minister, thought Emma: saying, don't worry: we won't allow this issue to become important.

But something made Emma turn and look at Marais, then follow his gaze back to the two Italians. He had seen the gesture and registered the body language. This has to be it she thought: his hidden agenda somehow involves Fede.

But the leprechaun was grinning with delight. He was remembering the rows provoked when his very own Pádraig Flynn, once the Commissioner for Social Affairs, complained that the Community's health policies were being totally undermined by the vast subsidies paid to tobacco farmers.

'There's been no suggestion so far as I'm aware,' he now said mischievously, 'that we cull tobacconists. Don't let's delude ourselves. We take decisions just as much on political grounds as on health ones. We do this all the time with tobacco and we did the same with BSE.'

The Spaniard, white with anger, looked as though he was about to throw up.

Phew, thought Emma. I did exceed my brief, but I was rescued.

However, she was not yet off the hook: the Belgian now spoke.

'So I take it that you believe the decision of your Minister – to ban beef on the bone – was unjustified.'

Damn him, damn him, Emma thought. Her hesitation was so obvious that the German reinforced the attack.

'Commissioner,' he said, 'a moment ago I observed that Madame Austen's conclusions were out of order. But too late – alas – she had already stated them. I insist she gives her opinion on this matter, too.'

They are doing this deliberately, thought Emma. Making potential trouble for me back home and for Marais here. She took a deep breath and looked straight at the speaker.

'I think it was unjustified on scientific grounds and mistaken on political ones. Once again my reasons have to do with the right of the public – who are not fools – to be allowed to decide what risks to take. The chances that a human infection could follow from eating beef on the bone are sixty times lower than that of a personal lightning strike. The public is permitted choice in situations where the risk is far, far higher. So why not here?'

Now everyone was looking at the UK Agriculture Minister. He said nothing; his face betrayed nothing. Marais' face too, was impassive but, my goodness Emma thought admiringly, he knows what he is about, all right. True – no one had mentioned fraud, but then it wasn't on the agenda.

As they rose, Marais turned to Emma and touched her lightly on the shoulder.

'Thank you very much,' and gave her an affectionate smile. She never forgot that look.

CHAPTER ELEVEN

Playing out the Farce

Then he died, saying 'bring down the curtain the farce is played out.'

François Rabelais: *attributed last words*

As he waited for his guests in his exclusive dining-room on the twelfth floor, the President was reflective. Only a few weeks remained till he would leave the Commission and become a Parliamentarian. Though he, and the Commissioners he led, had been forced – by colleagues and circumstances – to resign, at least he could acknowledge some of his successes with a series of valedictory lunches. The lifting of the beef ban throughout Europe was surely just a few weeks away; his endorsement of a distinguished political economist from France as the new – albeit temporary – Agriculture Commissioner had been politically very astute. The French were exceedingly pleased.

How convenient then that Charles Marais had convened a meeting to discuss some report or other – he wasn't quite sure what. The conjunction was irresistible. The Commissioner and the Agriculture Ministers were coming to lunch.

The food was exquisite, the compliments flattering. Then, with dessert finished and champagne poured, he rose to his feet and with his characteristic benevolent smile, prepared to offer a toast. But as he said '*Mes chers amis,*' he heard a gasp, then an alarming choke.

To his left the UK Agricultural Minister heard it too. He stared across the table, then watched aghast at the sudden clutch at the chest, the sweat pouring off the skin, the draining of colour from the face – each symptom following on in dreadful slow motion. As a lethal pallor exerted its final dominance, Marais' eyes fixed on the British Minister with a gaze so angry and intense that it seemed to reach out and grab him.

Then with a scattering of cutlery and smashing of plates, the body fell forward. Marais' flailing arm swept the champagne glass to the floor and his head came to rest in the *béhanzin* – the exquisite dessert that the Chief Chef of the President's Dining-Room had made that very morning.

Later some unkind people, who really should have known better, remarked distastefully that the British had finally taken dreadful revenge – though why on Marais? Others attributed the appalled expression on the face of the UK Minister to a fear – well-founded as it turned out – that the media would be unable to resist the headlines.

DEATH OF AGRICULTURE COMMISSIONER
BRITISH BEEF SERVED AT CELEBRATORY LUNCH

The war would begin again and not even the most skilled of spin doctors could prevent it.

There was controlled pandemonium. Aides, urgently summoned, rushed in, swept everyone out and discussed the next step – how to remove Marais from Breydel without anyone noticing, especially the journalists who would still be hanging around after the daily press conference. If they caught even a glimpse of a body being bundled out of the main entrance, God knows what would be in the evening editions. The Head of Security was told to come up with a suggestion – fast.

'There is a car park on the corner of Rue Belliard, with a separate entrance into Breydel. Take him down there.'

'Are you sure no one will see?'

'No I'm not sure, but it's the best I can do. Make your choice: it's either the main entrance or the car park.'

The hospital, Clinique du Parc Léopold, was close and within minutes their paramedics were racing through the corridors to the dining-room. They quickly inserted an IV line and fitted an oxygen mask over the grey face. But theirs were grim. Still, they took Marais down fast and though the paramedics couldn't have cared less whether anyone saw, the President's aides were confident that no one had even spotted the ambulance, let alone anything as untoward as a dead Commissioner.

Out of the car park, the ambulance turned right down Rue Belliard, then moved over to take the first left at the traffic lights. But the radio crackled.

'All right; all right!' they responded impatiently. 'We're on our way. We'll be there in two minutes.'

The instructions came back very firmly.

'You are not, repeat not, to come in the main entrance. Go on down Rue Belliard to the second set of lights, turn left into the Chaussée d'Etterbeek.'

'But that's a one-way street against us!'

'Don't argue. Do it and come in at the back.'

CHAPTER TWELVE

The Centre Gives Way

*Cannon-balls may aid the truth
But thought's a weapon stronger
We'll win our battles by its aid;
Wait a little longer.*

Charles Mackay: *The Good Time Coming*

Emma returned to the Conference Room well ahead of time. She needed to recoup. If the morning's meeting had been bad the afternoon's could likely be worse. She was greatly surprised when at thirty minutes before its start, the door opened and Felice Fede came into the room. But he seemed subdued, his usual cheery face strained.

'Madame Austen...' he stammered and stopped.

'Yes, Dr Fede?' Emma smiled encouragingly.

Fede pulled up a chair and sat down, heavily.

'Madame Austen.' He tried again.

What's wrong, thought Emma. He didn't shoot his cuffs.

'I'm afraid I've some terrible news. Commissioner Marais collapsed suddenly at lunch and...'

Emma felt her colour drain away. Her 'Oh no!' drowned out Fede's...died.'

'I'm afraid so. A heart attack.'

She stood up. Fede remained seated.

'But it's not possible!' She had been talking to him only two hours ago. He couldn't have just left.

Fede now rose.

'Our meeting this afternoon is cancelled, of course. The Ministers and the others have all left. The President is informing the French Ambassador and I have some urgent matters to settle. I'm meeting with the *cabinet* shortly. But please come and see us before you leave – at half past three perhaps?'

'Of course.'

'I'd be grateful.'

For a few moments Emma simply shuffled papers around aimlessly as, struggling for control, she tried to impose order on her racing thoughts.

How quickly life could change. Bolts flung by fate dropped from clear blue skies. Nothing could be taken for granted; nothing was certain; it was ever thus. She felt again the pain of her father's abrupt departure and the betrayal by her American lover. The scar tissue was still not thick enough.

Then head in hands, once more she shivered, for again the ghost was walking on her grave.

At half past three she entered the room. Felice Fede and Willi Dashöfer, deep in conversation in one corner, acknowledged her presence with polite nods. The remainder of the *cabinet* were clustered together, talking nervously. Céline Bardot, her face red and blotched, was very distressed. Sybilla Høgstrøm might appear the epitome of Olympian calm, but she was white-faced as she came forward and took Emma by both hands.

'This is terrible – quite terrible,' she murmured.

Like pallbearers, the Musketeers solemnly inclined their heads towards Emma, almost in unison but not quite.

Now Céline came forward, embraced Emma and started to cry again.

Emma sensed the atmosphere was taut. With the extinction of Marais' life the cords binding them to a common loyalty were fraying fast. The two older members of the *cabinet* may have been coping with detachment, but the Musketeers were betraying their youth with nervous bravado.

'I wonder what's going to happen now?' said one, staring at Emma.

'Does it really matter?' said Arthos. 'We're all finished here. There will be a new Commissioner and a new *cabinet*.'

He had always been a touch cynical, though would describe himself as just realistic. But now there was a brutality in his voice.

'And you'll return to Paris, won't you?' said Céline with bitterness in hers. Arthos shrugged.

'But, of course. We would have returned anyway in due course, unlike some I know,' looking pointedly at Sybilla.

'But what about his vision?' said the third Musketeer. 'Could the Commissioner have carried all before him?'

'We'll never know now,' said the other Musketeer sadly. But I often wondered. Did he realise how high the political price would be for the openness he wanted? One was paid for the beef truce, all right.'

'What price was paid?' interjected Emma quietly.

'Well, you of all people should guess. The quid pro quo is obvious. Britain would agree to press on with joining the euro in return for a rapid winding down of German opposition. Though it didn't quite work out, a scientist could plot a neat correlating graph. Couldn't they?' he challenged.

'I'm not quite that cynical,' Emma observed.

'Perhaps it would be better if we all were. The truth is never admitted, but the Commissioner knew where it lay.'

Another devastated young man, controlling himself by showing off, his voice was close to breaking as he continued.

'The breakthrough in the beef war began with the lifting of the ban in Ulster. Why there? Because farmers had computer records, tracing the lineage and movements of every cow back for eight years. The official line was that these were introduced as an anti-BSE measure. Not on your life. They were the only weapon available to combat a lovely fraud.'

'What on earth are you talking about?' Céline was thoroughly provoked. Her hands were still: she let her hair droop across her eyes. Arthos took up the story.

'Oh, that was one of the biggest rackets of all time. The Irish Republic did very nicely out of the Common Agricultural Policy, thank you, with huge subsidies for every head of cattle. But some people quickly realised that the neatest way to increase the subsidies was to increase the numbers and the neatest way to increase the numbers was to bootleg the animals. Every time they crossed and recrossed the border with Ulster, someone collected an export subsidy in addition. In the end they probably didn't even bother to move the cows. You could pretend they existed. Just like olive trees.'

But, now a Nordic ice-maiden advanced on Arthos. Sybilla was furiously angry.

'What precisely do you know about such matters?' she asked. Her voice was frigid and she glared at him.

'Everyone knows these things happen all over our sector,' he replied, somewhat lamely.

'No, that's simply not true,' protested Céline, warmly.

'I asked what precisely *you* know about it all,' Sybilla repeated, still towering over the young man.

If I was Arthos, thought Emma, I'd be scared and I'd duck. But he wasn't and he didn't.

'Fraud in DG VI isn't anything new. It's in the public record. We all know the Commissioner felt very strongly about it.'

'Did he discuss fraud with you?' demanded Sybilla, 'You've not been here long. I want to know.'

In the face of her onslaught, Arthos' cool seemed to desert him. 'Oh, very little,' he stammered.

Well, that's a lie for a start, thought Emma. Generally he expressed his energy with darting eyes, laughter and restless movement of loose limbs. Now he was ramrod-straight and very still.

'Well, you shouldn't go round talking about matters of which you are totally ignorant,' said Sybilla and released him. So far as she was concerned Arthos had been well and truly put in his place.

Emma eyed them both. He won't leave well alone, she guessed. A Musketeer has his Gallic pride after all – and they really dislike each other. What had they in common, save Marais? His indispensable aide versus his indispensable mistress. And just how indispensable had she been?

'Well, God help us all, it's history now,' Arthos spoke softly, with a touch of despair, not yet ready to face the irrevocable fact of death. 'Whatever battles the Commissioner was fighting he was bound to lose. For the structure here inevitably leads to corruption. Perhaps it's best to go along with everything since you can't change anything. In any case, what's a few thousand cows or a million euros between friends?'

'If this is your attitude you shouldn't ever have come to Brussels.' Céline's voice was cold.

He shrugged.

'I've no doubt you will prosper greatly in your career,' she continued bitterly.

'I fully intend to – and without parachuting.'

'Parachuting?' queried Emma.

'A parachutist is someone who drops in from outside into a permanent plum job that's not deserved. Many people do this.' And he glared again at Sybilla.

'I didn't entirely sympathise with what the Commissioner was trying to do over public accountability,' commented the third Musketeer. 'It was surprising in an *énarque*. Surely he realised that any such initiative was bound to fail.'

'Is that why you lot always say accountability is unnecessary?' queried Arthos.

'Of course. According to our philosophy it's both irrelevant and unnecessary. Even Commissioner Kinnock once publicly admitted that such accountability as exists in the College is entirely voluntary – and he's British, for God's sake.'

'Whenever did he say that?' asked Emma. Perhaps she shouldn't encourage the conversation given the circumstances, but she was intrigued.

'During a BBC radio series called *The Eurocrats*. I heard him being interviewed – in 1996 I think – when I was being briefed about Brussels. He said the obligation he felt as Commissioner was far stronger than when accountability was compulsory – as it was when he was Leader of the Opposition. The interviewer didn't sound at all convinced – and anyway not everyone here shares Kinnock's lofty sense of moral purpose. And what can we do about them?'

Hmm! thought Emma. I seem to recall Neil Kinnock, along with all the other Commissioners, retreating under the collegiate umbrella during the latest row. If you dare fire one, you must fire us all.

'But why couldn't Commissioner Marais realise his vision?' she asked.

'Because everything that happens here is both irrevocable and unaccountable. First, because there is no mechanism whereby actions of the general public can repeal EU laws or overturn directives. Secondly, though the Parliament might want to fire individual Commissioners for incompetence, sexual deviance or political misdeeds, they still can't – even if they had the guts to try again, which frankly I doubt. Don't forget Prodi says he will not allow them to fire individual Commissioners.'

'But he extracted a personal promise from each one to resign if he asks,' objected a Musketeer.

'I don't think that will work either. They'll hang together,' said Arthos. 'Prodi's intentions may be good but the basic system will never change. Look, it's not the Commissioners who are the real problem. They come and go. But the top bureaucracy remains.'

'But the European Court of Justice could get rid of the lot,' said the Musketeer again.

'There you *énarques* go again, being totally theoretical. Anyway, that would take forever by which time they'd have all left anyway. The Commission is so secure that no one ever has to admit there's been a mistake – not that they ever make them, of course.'

'But that's the very reason.' Céline turned to them with a terrible, passionate earnestness, 'why we, who work permanently in the House, must strive to ensure that we make the right decisions. We are taking them on behalf of millions of European citizens. We knew from the beginning that ours is a heavy responsibility.' She was pleading now. 'And that's why you shouldn't regard time here as just a step up the rung of your personal career ladder.'

But Arthos seemed intent on needling Céline.

'Why are you so high-minded? You didn't agree with the Commissioner on openness.'

No, you certainly didn't, agreed Emma silently. I had to chisel the stuff out of you.

Céline looked even more distressed and made no move to straighten her hair. 'I didn't enjoy disagreeing with him on anything.'

Which, Emma wondered, as she listened to the exchange, was the most dangerous? Devil-may-care cynicism or omniscient idealism? She knew that Sybilla maintained a third way – an hereditary disdain for the masses. And did Arthos really believe what he was saying, or had the black hole of eternity completely unnerved him?

Fortunately, Felice Fede and Willie Dashöfer now came over. The three young men immediately calmed down and appeared appropriately deferential.

'I am so sorry to have kept you waiting, Madame Austen,' said Fede formally. He was happily shooting his cuffs again. 'There's much to sort out and it will be some weeks before a new Commissioner can be appointed. Meantime we've got to deal with the press release and similar matters.'

The word 'press' jolted Emma. My God, she said to herself, I should have thought of this earlier. She interrupted Fede's formal: '...so thank you for all you have done and now...'

'What were they eating at lunch?' she asked abruptly.

He stared at her in astonishment, as if she were slightly mad. Dashöfer gave her his bristly glare.

'Of what possible importance could this be?' said Céline. She was weeping again. Amongst the voices of the others, Emma latched on to Sybilla Høgstrøm.

'Brandade, beef and *béhanzin*.'

'What did you say?' chorused the Musketeers.

Sybilla assumed an importantly professional air, reflecting competent insider knowledge. 'Well, brandade is a mousse of salt cod served with olives – a speciality from Provence. It makes an excellent starter for a meal.'

'So what?'

'And *béhanzin* is a rare speciality from Tunisia – an Arabic cake.'

How on Earth do you know so precisely what they had for lunch? thought Emma. Then she remembered the telephone call she'd overheard the first time she was at Avenue Fond'roy. If Sybilla was one of the most famous cooks in Brussels, the President's chef, Antoine, was another. Apparently the two regularly swapped recipes, discussed menus, exchanged dishes and enjoyed a friendship which, in a city of avid and sometimes prurient gossip, no one had ever suggested was anything but purely culinary.

'Did you say beef?' Emma heard herself asking. The question echoed round her head: beef, beef. Oh God!

'Yes, indeed.' Céline was speaking. 'I know that beef was to be served. Since the lunch was celebrating the easing of the ban, serving beef was entirely appropriate.'

Emma didn't like what she had to do.

'What kind of beef? Where did it come from?'

'What on Earth does this matter?'

'Tell me. Where did it come from?' Her voice was rough.

Once again, Céline answered. 'British beef, of course. We wanted to make this gesture and...'

'Oh, no!' Arthos had made the connection Emma was about to point out.

'Well,' she commented brutally, 'if everyone in Brussels knows what they had for lunch, then you'd better watch out for the headlines in tomorrow's newspapers.'

Both Fede and Dashöfer looked shocked and Céline reacted angrily.

'Emma, I think your remark is thoroughly distasteful considering the circumstances.'

'Yes, it is,' agreed Emma, 'but I'm warning you. The press will find it irresistible.'

There was a stunned silence.

'She's right,' said Sybilla.

'I hope not,' said Fede, 'But...'

'She's right.' Sybilla said again. 'We should take immediate steps to quash dangerous rumours.'

'Spin doctors?' murmured Arthos, laconically.

Fede glared at him and tried to take control. 'Madame Austen, you have worked a great deal with the media. Should we get a statement from the doctors or the hospital or something?'

'I think you should get an official medical bulletin issued very quickly. And there must be no ambiguity about the cause of the Commissioner's death.'

'Of course we must.' Sybilla yet again.

'Thank goodness,' Fede continued, 'we don't have any immediate problems other than coming to terms with this dreadful tragedy. The Commissioner was taking a few days off and as usual had set everything in good order. So there's nothing else that can't wait.'

But, Emma suddenly remembered, there was something that absolutely couldn't wait. Starting tomorrow, Marais was indeed taking a few days off – going to Northern Italy with his son, Thierry. She glanced at her watch – four o'clock. She had been asked to join them at six o'clock. The odds were that in complete ignorance of what had happened, Marais' son was already in Brussels waiting for his father to return home.

The drive out to the top end of the Avenue Louise and the Square du Bois was far too long for comfort. Marais' death consumed her. At one level she was grappling with the puzzle of why. What had been wrong with him? At another she was wondering how to handle the encounter. She had never in her life broken tragic news to anyone and just hoped she could hit the right note of sensitivity and unambiguity.

At the top of the Avenue, elegant shops gave way to elegant houses. Then suddenly the trees of the Bois de la Cambre lay straight ahead. The taxi swung right around a large stone plinth, bearing a large statue of rearing horses and two warriors in a close combat. Green stains dripped down. They stopped at the entrance to a small square, barred by high metal gates and barriers across the roadway.

The driver shrugged: she had to walk. Emma was glad of any time before she must meet Charles Marais' son so, delaying as long as possible, she took her bearings, registering every detail in painful clarity. On the railing between the two entrances to the Square – one in, one out – a blue plaque proclaimed Square du Bois. Underneath, for those whose French was poor, it proclaimed Bois Square. Beneath the plaque was a small postbox.

Walking carefully over the cobbled stones, Emma searched for the house. On each side some nine houses were set along a line that curved gently to a natural end – a large tree, in full leaf. The houses were elegant enough, but there was no uniformity of style. Some were of red brick, others white stone, most had wrought iron balconies. The entrance of one was guarded by two stone lions, with the front door and windows heavily barred. Somehow she guessed this wasn't Marais' residence.

She had to walk almost to the very end until she found the small house of three floors. In stylish contrast to the uniform flatness of the others, its façade was an elegant curve.

She hesitated and looked up. At the top, rectangular windows – of a bedroom, perhaps? – opened onto a large curved iron balcony protected by the slope of the roof. The three French windows of the next floor were tall, thin and a smaller balcony adorned the central window, though all were set off by wrought iron window-boxes with flowers. The shutters of the ground floor windows were half open.

A small box hedge separated the path to the front door from the stone terrace of the neighbouring house with its carriage lantern. Two small green trees to the left had either just been recently planted, or weren't doing very well.

Taking a deep breath, she walked along the path, up two steps and pressed the bell. She heard footsteps running down the stairs, then the door opened. Standing in front of her was a young man of about thirty-five years, in smart canvas trousers and a faded indigo polo shirt, that held the logo, 'Grootbos Nature Reserve'. He's been to South Africa, she thought.

He had been reading and his spectacles were pushed up onto a head of thick, dark wavy hair. He looked so like his father that Emma felt faint. The same high forehead, oval face with good bone structure, blue-grey eyes, laughter lines at the corners. He looked at her intently and she could almost see the thought processes spinning in his head.

'You must be Dr Austen,' he decided finally. 'My father told me that you were joining us this evening. But I'm afraid he's not yet back. Please come up.'

He took her coat and, with a courteous apology for going first, led the way to the large drawing-room upstairs. As Emma entered the room, her eyes were immediately drawn to a formal French tapestry on the wall that had to be very old – seventeenth or eighteenth century perhaps. The landscape showed two groups of trees each side with small birds perched on branches; a river ran down the middle and a castle was set in the central background – the seat of the family who had commissioned the work. At centre right and centre left, two large birds, woven more naïvely, were standing face to face, very formally. The colours – green, blue, brown, gold and ivory – were discreet and charming though at two points the grassland was touched soft pink.

A bookcase containing leather-bound books and two delicate tables holding bronze and ivory objects, added a touch of austerity to the room. But this was relieved by warm Persian rugs, a Regency cabriolet with cushions and an extremely comfortable sofa of Italian design. At the end of the room away from the street, a panelled folding doorway led to what obviously was a study. The general atmosphere was of understated taste and wealth.

As Thierry gestured her towards the sofa, Emma drew a deep breath but remained standing.

'May I ask the maid to get you something?' he enquired, pulling up a chair. 'Tea, a cool drink? Something stronger?'

Again, Emma took a deep breath. 'Dr Marais...' she began.

'Thierry,' he prompted, as they sat down.

But Emma still waited, then thought with sad horror: Oh God, I've heard these same words already today.

'Thierry,' she repeated gently, 'I'm afraid I've some terrible news. Your father collapsed suddenly at lunch and died. We believe he had a heart attack.'

There was a long silence. He remained still, yet Emma saw the clenched hands.

'I am so very sorry.'

Finally he spoke: 'I do not understand. This cannot be.'

Again, an identical denial.

'I'm afraid so,' said Emma. 'I came to find you because I knew you were travelling to Brussels this afternoon and I didn't want you to hear the news on the radio. I don't think your father's colleagues knew you were en route.'

'That was most kind of you. Where is he? Where did they take him?'

'I'm afraid I don't know. But I do know that the French Embassy was informed.'

Thierry got up, sat down, then rose again with a look of such sadness on his face that Emma's heart ached.

'Of course. I will call the Ambassador. Will you excuse me, please? Let me see that you have some tea or something, anyway.'

He went out of the room. She heard him go down the stairs and then voices in the kitchen. Then he returned: 'It's coming.' He crossed the long width of the room and went through the panelled folding doors leading to Marais' study. Emma caught sight of a desk and on the wall above, a mediaeval painting of two women's faces possibly? This had to be the Fra Angelico copy that Marais had mentioned. The expression of suffering was terribly poignant.

The voice in the study rose and fell. The maid – a Moroccan – brought in a tray. Then, after some five minutes, Thierry returned. As she heard the phone go down Emma had risen to pour his tea.

'Thank you,' he said 'The Ambassador confirmed the news. My father is at the hospital. I'm afraid I will have to go over and complete some formalities.'

He sat down again, his face still white and pained. 'Dr Austen.'

'Emma, please.'

'I cannot take this in. I simply cannot believe this has happened. My father never had a day's illness in his life.'

'That was my reaction,' she said gently, pulling at her scarf a little. 'I had dinner with him last night and he was in wonderful form.'

'I knew you were dining together. My father called a couple of days ago to say he was asking you round this evening. He thought I would like to meet you.'

He had it all planned, thought Emma, again with amused affection.

'Well, he gave me a wonderful evening. He was so looking forward to going to Italy with you.'

'So was I. We often went there – as a family' – clutching at a familiar past, before it was erased forever. 'The first time I was about ten and spent my days racing through the countryside. But I also remember that my father took us down to Arrezo so he could browse in the antique shops. I was bored out of my skull and my mother was cross with me for my bad manners.'

He finished his tea, stood up again and said. 'I must go.'

Emma caught a glimpse of the boy, now desolate, and on impulse said: 'Would you like me to come with you?'

'Would you? I'd be most grateful.'

The drive, practically back to Breydel, took a silent half hour. As they walked into the lobby of the hospital, a young man came forward – another of the many charming young Frenchmen in Brussels – fair haired, elegantly suited, he was trained to be diplomatic however stressful the circumstances. He offered Thierry softly spoken words of condolence. The Ambassador had instructed him to say that Dr Marais should feel free to call for any assistance, at any time. Perhaps he would care to come to the Embassy at his convenience? Finally he turned back to the desk and spoke to the receptionist. She dialled a number on the phone and soon after a doctor appeared.

The doctor must have been about the same age as Thierry, Emma thought, but he looked far older. Thinning hair, tired, careworn eyes reflected a long day and probably long night on duty and a sense of never having come to terms with the heart-rending aspects of his profession. The stethoscope, folded and stuffed into the right hand pocket of his white coat, hung as limply as his left hand – both like rag dolls, Emma thought unhappily. The aura of mortality surrounded him, yet he was both matter of fact and sensitive. Probably that was the point where he became torn. She hoped he had a wonderful wife and happy children at home.

'I'm Robert Dewiere,' he said as they shook hands. 'I had the sad duty to examine your father when he arrived. May I ask you to come this way?'

Thierry turned to Emma with a look that was both questioning and faintly imploring.

115

'Of course,' she murmured and went with them.

She had not been in a mortuary before and thanked God Thierry didn't have to see the body in a drawer, being pulled out of cold storage. Marais was on a table. As the sheet was drawn back, Thierry stepped forward and waited a moment. Emma was fighting back her tears. Then, with great dignity and composure Thierry turned to Dewiere and said, 'Yes, that is my father.' He leant over, kissed Marais' forehead, waited for another silent minute, then turned away.

Outside the door he was still not quite in total control but carried a look of great resolution.

'Dr Dewiere,' he said, 'What was wrong with my father?'

'He had a heart attack.'

'But why?'

'I don't honestly know,' said Dewiere. 'Many things provoke sudden cardiac arrest. Stress – maybe a blood clot. Did he smoke? I know nothing about his lifestyle. You will understand that this is the first time I had ever seen him.'

'No, he didn't smoke,' said Thierry, 'and he kept active and watched his diet carefully. I've never known him have a moment's illness in his life. He had a great sense of humour and handled stress well. I know that makes him sound immortal but I find his death totally incomprehensible.'

The tears were pricking behind Emma's eyes. Oh, so do I, she wanted to say.

'Well, I'm extremely sorry,' said Dewiere. 'It's very sad. Please let me know what you want us to do.'

'Dr Marais,' said the young man from the Embassy, 'we are of course, at your disposal to help you make whatever arrangements you wish. You will, I am sure, be wanting to return to France.'

'Of course,' said Thierry, 'my father will be buried in the Auvergne. But, forgive me, I think I will go home now. I'll be in touch in the morning.'

'Of course. The Embassy car will take you back.'

Thierry turned again to Emma. This time there was no question in his eyes, but a quiet assumption that she would be coming too. Again he was silent during the long drive. Back at the house, with Emma settled upstairs, he went down to the kitchen and shortly afterwards she heard the maid weeping. Then Thierry returned to the drawing-room.

'May I offer you a drink?' he said. 'Whisky?'

Emma needed one badly. 'Please.'

'Malt,' he said, 'or the ordinary stuff?'

'Malt, and no ice, thank you. Just a little water.'

He poured out two generous measures and as he carried them over murmured, 'It's always like this. I simply can't take it in. Just as before.'

Emma, watching his face, realised that the words 'just as before' referred to the death of his fiancée. Just as sudden, just as unexpected, the news likely brought by a stranger. There was a sense of unreality, a brutal severance from everyday life, which persisted in continuing in all its small, regular details. Yet the bereaved felt total disjunction as time screeched to a sudden, grinding halt.

'I'd like to show you something,' said Thierry.

She followed him into the study. There was nothing as fancy as a computer on Marais' large Georgian desk – only a blotter, an old-fashioned ink stand, some files and photographs. He stopped underneath the painting on the wall which she had glimpsed earlier.

'That's the painting my father found when we took that holiday in Tuscany.'

'It's a copy of a Fra Angelico, isn't it?' said Emma.

He turned and looked at her with Marais' lovely smile. 'Yes, it is – part of his *Retable du Couronnement de la Vierge.* How did you know? Are you familiar with his paintings?'

'Not at all,' said Emma, 'but last night your father told me the family story – how he'd dragged you down to Arrezo,

117

where he found a grubby canvas which for all of a few moments he imagined was an original.'

'He did indeed. My sister and I teased him quite unmercifully. It is, of course, a nineteenth-century copy. The original was first in the church of San Domenico in Fiesole, but in 1812 it went to the Louvre. Wherever he was based my father always had this with him.'

'Who are the two women?' asked Emma.

'No one's really sure. The Virgin is probably one and the saint in blue is possibly Mary Magdalene, except that she's carrying her head far too high. She is generally shown in a far more humble mien – head down and all that.'

'Are you Catholic?' asked Emma.

'Lapsed – very lapsed. Nevertheless my father was a spiritual man, though he believed in the substance rather than the symbols.'

'What did he find so appealing about Fra Angelico's work?'

'The man for a start. Contemporaries said he was a person of gentle simplicity and saintly temperament, who led a calm, quiet life. It wasn't that my father wanted – or expected – such a life for himself, but the paintings formed a contemplative counterpoint to his busy schedule. I suppose the one element in him that did converge with Fra Angelico was his sense of tranquil acceptance.'

'I'm not certain I'd call tranquil acceptance a characteristic of your father,' observed Emma.

'No, indeed – nor of any of my family. We have always challenged self-satisfied people with comfortable assumptions. But that is not what I meant. Look at those two faces. Experience and suffering etched in every line, yet they reflect the peace of eternity.'

He was silent. Emma didn't want to think of eternity – too horribly final.

'I didn't manage to explain to Dr Dewiere at all well how my father handled stress. His sense of humour was just wonderful. He could always laugh – against himself and the human predicament. He was also fatalistic though not in the way that says it's all ordained so you don't have to act. More in the Ethiopian sense of "*desta*" – "fate" meaning "joy". This is what has happened, so you cope. "Be still and know that I am God." But as for me,' and he sighed, 'I don't think so. I don't know any longer if there are any eternal truths.'

Emma put her hand gently on his arm.

He turned to her as he had done earlier and said, 'I still don't believe it. Why? Just at this moment?'

He was speaking so calmly that his next words were a shock.

'I shall insist on a post-mortem.'

And as the ghost walked on her grave for a third and final time, Emma knew – just knew – there was something suspicious about Marais' death.

CHAPTER THIRTEEN

The Devil in the Detail

If ever I ate a good supper at night
I dream'd of the Devil and wak'd in a fright

Christopher Anstey: 'The New Bath Guide', *letter 4.*
A Consultation of the Physicians

By the end of the day Emma was exhausted, shattered by Marais' death, distressed by Thierry's sorrow. For most of the night she tossed restlessly. When in the white hours she finally dropped off, her sleep was invaded by a disturbing dream and fraud was the pervasive thread in its weird weavings.

The Director-General of DG VI, Charles Stewart, and Willie Dashöfer, had appropriated the entire annual budget of DG VI – forty billion, take a euro, leave a euro – and were en route to a Pacific hideaway along with herds of scrapie infected sheep. Then Thierry appeared in his capacity as Head of the Russian Mafia, insisting on his cut and all the sheep. Various anarchic episodes followed, ending with Sybilla Høgstrøm imprisoned in a tall tower and the Musketeers riding to her rescue. After a furious argument, Arthos rode off with her on a white horse. Why not me? thought Emma indignantly and woke up laughing.

For a few escapist moments the farcical hilarity of her dream was more real than the sadness of her conscious day.

Then she called down to reception for the papers. The headlines were just as she had feared. The conjunction of Marais' death with British beef was given due prominence. But Fede, too, had moved fast for an official hospital bulletin stated that Commissioner Marais had been pronounced dead of a heart attack on arrival at the hospital. Whose arm did Fede twist to get it out so quickly?

After breakfast she telephoned Jane and briefly told her what had happened. They talked little: Jane sensed her shock and Emma, Jane's support.

She decided to spend the morning working. The weather was grey, Brussels singularly unappealing. She had no wish to sightsee nor shop. She could have returned to Cambridge but was not ready to do so.

Wanting to see Thierry again, she supposed he was at the Embassy, insisting on a post-mortem. Then, poor man, he would have many disturbing matters to arrange, at once eminently practical and horribly final. She doubted whether she would ever see him again.

But at noon the telephone rang and he was apologising for disturbing her. He had called Breydel and DG VI, but had been told to try the hotel. He needed to see her urgently. Could he come over?

'Would you like me to come to you?'

'Thank you, but no,' he replied. 'I'm still at the Embassy. I'll be with you in fifteen minutes. We'll have lunch first.'

Sprucely dressed in a dark suit, he looked haggard and the pulse in his temple was throbbing. Bone tired, she thought: he can't have slept at all. But again, there was no mistaking Charles Marais' son. He came up quickly, kissed her hand as his father had done some thirty-six or so hours earlier and steered her out of the very same lobby. They walked round the corner to a simple restaurant and ordered omelettes, salad and dark Chimey beer. Thierry spoke – quite lightly at first – of how helpful the Ambassador had been and had she seen the newspapers and the official hospital bulletin, which was downright premature. But something else was preoccupying him, for during coffee he asked: 'Emma, what do you know about fraud?'

'I got very close to it once,' she replied. 'Components was the target of a Nigerian scam. Why do you want to know?'

But she knew what was coming.

'I'll tell you later. What happened in your case?'

'Well, one day we received a fax on Bank of Nigeria notepaper. The three writers claimed to be a high official from the Bank of Nigeria, an equally high one from the Ministry of Health and an exceedingly high one from the Treasury. They knew all about our work in Africa.

'They wrote that there was an underspend left over from Nigeria's health programmes amounting to a cool thirty million dollars. If Components would expedite the transfer of these funds to a bank in Europe, then we would receive a cut of some ten million dollars in the form of a certified Bank of Nigeria cheque, a photocopy of which they would provide –'

'But only if,' interrupted Thierry, 'you sent them four blank letterheads, signed by your Financial Officer, together with a pro forma invoice, details of your bank's address and your account number, so that they could deposit the money. But in practice they would actually extract yours. We get these all the time.'

'You have it exactly,' said Emma. 'We were about to tear it up but then the devil got in us.'

'Who's us?' asked Thierry.

'Me and my partner, Jane Acton. We knew it was a scam but we were both mad as hell that they were using the primary health care programmes in Nigeria as the basis of the fraud. So we strung them along by asking various pointed questions about the precise source of their funds. Then one day they had the gall to ring and in pained tones, say that they couldn't understand our delay. Could it be that we planned to shop them?'

'Was that it?'

'More or less. But I told the story to a friend – one-time Dean of Jesus College and a specialist in international fraud. "Let's lay this before the Nigerian High Commission," he said, though he could predict exactly what would happen.'

'So can I. Absolutely nothing after all. They tipped them off.'

'Very likely. That's the closest I have ever been to fraud.'

'Emma,' said Thierry seriously, 'My father was far, far closer. As you can imagine, I didn't sleep much last night. So I thought I should make a start on his papers. I came across a whole batch of notes taken after a meeting at UCLAF. He'd built up a dossier but was being careful to keep this out of the official filing system.'

Emma reached across the table and touched his hand.

'Before you go on, I should tell you that during our dinner, he said that problems like the beef crisis were not the worst he faced.'

'But...'

'His was fraud and he hated it. Afterwards I was surprised at his candour, because he was so discreet and never discussed the Directorate's affairs with me. But now I wonder: was this an index of how much the problem was troubling him?'

'Well,' observed Thierry, 'I know that he suspected people within his Directorate were directing fraud and it really was disturbing him.'

He paused for a moment.

'My father felt very angry about corruption – always had. Taxpayers carry an enormous burden anyway, without being fleeced a second time. Would you come back to the house and take a look at the notes? I didn't want to bring them with me.'

123

During this third, silent taxi ride Emma was reflective. Her own deep, intuitive suspicion – that Marais' death involved foul play – was utterly without foundation and she wouldn't share this with Thierry. But did he nurse similar suspicions? Yet why should he?

They were at the top end of the Avenue Louise before Thierry spoke.

'Why didn't your parents call you Jane?'

Emma laughed, her chain of thought well and truly broken.

'Well, they easily might, for they adored Jane Austen. But I am glad they didn't – far too great a burden. However, I admit, that along with every other woman in England, I thrilled at the sight of Colin Firth as Mr Darcy, emerging from the lake at Pemberley with clinging wet breeches.'

'Does it have to be a lake? Wouldn't a swimming pool do?'

'Absolutely not,' insisted Emma firmly.

'Well,' he said 'we have both at our place in the Auvergne.'

Now what could he possibly mean by that? thought Emma.

Once in Marais' study, under the gaze of the Fra Angelico, Thierry opened the top drawer of the desk and handed her a file.

'Take a look at this,' he invited.

Settled in a comfortable chair, Emma began reading, but within two minutes spoke.

'Well, one thing is now obvious. This squares precisely with an exchange that occurred yesterday afternoon amongst the Musketeers.'

'The what?'

'There are three young Frenchmen in the *cabinet,* nicknamed the Three Musketeers. One of them – Arthos – had a furious spat with Sybilla Høgstrøm.'

ROTTEN AT THE CORE

'My father's mistress.'

'Yes. When he mentioned your father's concern about fraud, she jumped on him so ferociously that he backed off. I wondered if your father had been discussing this with Arthos, or was Sybilla just defending her ground? These people get very territorial, you know. And,' she glanced down at the notes, 'Fede's all over the file and my God, Sybilla appears to have been shopping him.'

'You'll see my father suspected him. But why...?'

Thierry rose and walked restlessly around the room. Then he stopped in front of the painting, looked at it for a moment before turning back to her.

'Emma, I know I'm being irrational but why do I feel such foreboding?'

'Not at all,' she said trying to sound reassuring. 'The last hours have been dreadful and it's happened to you twice in as many years. So your feelings are utterly valid.'

'Thank you. I am finding it very hard.'

She returned to the file. The lawyer in her said it was an excellent brief. Marais had laid out a detailed case, separating the facts he knew from the evidence he had found from the suspicions he'd been fed. He identified not only what he didn't know but why he didn't know it. He obviously believed he was close to a source of fraud in DG VI and his case was compelling.

As she read, she occasionally sighed. When she sighed, Thierry looked up taking comfort at the sight of the elegant figure in the armchair, reading with intent concentration.

After half an hour, he sensed that she was finishing. She sighed gently again, loosened her scarf and her hand went up to rub her eyes.

'Drink? Same as yesterday?'

'Please.' Emma rose, stretched and put the file back on the desk.

125

Thierry went into the salon and she heard the chink of glasses. Then his footsteps receded and she guessed he had gone to fetch water. As she heard him return the phone rang. He came into the study and picked up the receiver.

'Thierry Marais,' he announced. Then his face went impassive.

She heard 'Yes,' and then 'Yes' again. Then he said nothing more for about two minutes, until his final, 'Thank you very much for letting me know.'

Then he turned and faced her.

'That was Robert Dewiere,' he said. 'The post-mortem revealed no cardiac failure, nor heart disease, nor circulatory problems – nothing like that at all.'

CHAPTER FOURTEEN

The Serpent on the Rock

Eine Krähe hackt der anderen kein Auge aus

German proverb: *One crow does not peck out the eye of another*

As Thierry handed her the glass Emma knew the moment had arrived when she would have to come clean.

'So,' Thierry said, 'we know how my father didn't die. But how *did* he? The hospital will say nothing for the time being.'

Nor ever, thought Emma – nor the Commission either.

She stood and, as formally as the two birds in the tapestry, they faced each other.

'Look,' she said, 'I've made things difficult for you. You and Dewiere are between a rock and a hard place.'

'Why do you say that?'

'Well, the announcement was partly my fault. Yesterday, when I was with the *cabinet,* I asked about the lunch menu. Everyone knew that British beef had been served. But I knew what a field-day the journalists would have when they found out. They would say that the Commissioner's death proved that our beef is still unsafe. When Dr Fede asked for my advice, I said a medical bulletin should be immediately issued. I wanted to cut off any media hares.'

'Hares?' He was baffled.

'English figure of speech. Fede swung into action fast. I was astonished when I saw the bulletin in this morning's papers.'

'But now we are truly boxed in,' observed Thierry, ruefully. 'It's not only that the hospital wouldn't want to admit they'd been wrong, but if they did, the tabloids could really go to town on the dangers of beef.'

He pulled at his lip thoughtfully.

'Oh, God. We can't possibly go public. But at least three things are ruled out. My father didn't die of a heart attack, nor of nvCJD, nor from food poisoning. Fifteen people were at the lunch, all ate the same menu and everyone else is just fine. So what's the explanation?'

'What about your father's medical records?' asked Emma 'Would his physician know anything?'

'Most unlikely. I'm not certain who this was, or even if he had one. Papa was totally useless to the medical profession – not even a healthy hypochondriac, as most Frenchmen love to be. I can recall only one occasion when he was out of sorts – a digestive upset or something, after an official lunch, when he was on a mission. So why does a man just die? Were you aware of any stress?'

'Nothing overwhelming. Of course, I've sensed the political battles – not so much with his aides, but the committees. People reacted angrily to your father's perceived post-mortem on the beef war at the meeting yesterday. Others hated my conclusion that we don't yet know whether eating beef is the route whereby people become infected, because in that case wrong decisions have been taken.'

'And they could have egg on their faces?'

'Yes. And besides, most of the *cabinet* disagreed with his intention to make decisions more open. He was a loose cannon they hadn't managed to tie down.'

'And fraud?' prompted Thierry.

'Well, that's another matter entirely, but echoes are reverberating. If your father was getting near to the source of fraud within DG VI, Fede – anyone – who had insider information linked to organised crime, would feel anxious. The knowledge could be lethal.'

Thierry latched directly on to the word. 'Lethal for whom?'

His thoughts were fast converging on her suspicions. Yet that is all they were – just suspicions. Everything – intuition, the ghost walking on her grave, the facts she had learnt in Brussels – might convince her that Marais had been in danger, but still she could not bring herself to say: I believe your father was murdered.

'Emma, please.'

Suddenly she felt hot and loosened her scarf from her neck. She liked this young man – oh, so much – just as she had his father.

'Thierry: I just don't know, but I wonder. Shortly after I arrived I learned from two impeccable sources – a journalist and someone in UCLAF – that your father had publicly demonstrated his determination to stamp out fraud within the Directorate. He'd also had a private meeting with one of the Examining Magistrates at UCLAF – a man called LeQuesne – and took care that everyone knew this had taken place. I was intrigued but my friends told me to stay clear.'

'Why?'

'Because they said it is dangerous to be interested in fraud in Brussels. Still, I've never been able to put that entirely out of my mind.'

Willing him to agree, she put her hand on his arm. 'But you see, it's inconceivable, isn't it? People don't go around murdering each other in the sacred hallways of Breydel, do they?'

Thierry's smile reflected amusement and ruefulness. Then his face set.

'Well, let's find out. Let's just analyse this. God knows, between us we've enough experience.'

How incredibly sensible, Emma thought as he pulled up another chair and, side by side, they sat at Marais' desk. Above, the saints in the Fra Angelico painting gazed down.

Emma glanced up. Tell us, she prayed, please tell us.

'Okay,' Thierry began, 'either my father died of natural causes or he did not. If he did, then eventually more details from the post-mortem and his own medical history should tell us why.'

'Not necessarily,' objected Emma. She would play this in advocate style. 'And there are two reasons. First you believe that no medical records exist; secondly, it's not at all certain that further details from the post-mortem will tell us anything new. Some conditions remain hidden. What tests did they do?'

'I don't know. I could insist on a full range being done though I'd rather not unless we have some idea of what to look for.'

'And,' said Emma, 'if nothing turned up they'd still take refuge in the standard ploy – heart failure of unknown origin. Still, blood samples will have been retained.'

'So then, the next step.'

Emma took a deep breath.

'Well, if we are prepared to consider that your father died from unnatural causes we've a whole different set of questions to answer. How did he die; who killed him; what possibly could be their motive?'

'Which question is the best one to start with?' asked Thierry with genuine curiosity.

Emma sighed. 'Quite frankly, I haven't the slightest idea. I've never done this before. But if there's a motive, we'll find it somewhere in that dossier and if he suspected someone, then that person becomes our chief suspect. But this is too amateur for words.'

Thierry interrupted. 'If we identify a likely suspect, this won't automatically lead to the method will it.'

'It might but probably not. And we've no smoking guns, no dripping daggers, no people leaping into small offices in Breydel and strangling bureaucrats.'

'What a pity,' murmured Thierry drily. 'At the moment everything, but everything,' and his frustration was now plain, 'is leading absolutely nowhere. Nothing makes any sense.'

'So we only have two ways to go.'

'And they are?'

'First, we must collect every scrap of evidence we can and hope a pattern emerges.'

'But this of itself won't lead to the answer, will it?' objected Thierry.

'Not at all, only to further questions – the why questions. But it's a good method. Detectives and scientists use it all the time.'

'And the second way?' Thierry's question pulled her back from her thoughts.

'Start with a hypothesis…' she hesitated and sighed, 'but this isn't going to get us anywhere either. We don't have one!'

Now Thierry sighed.'How true: the only hypothesis we have is that maybe my father died unnaturally. *Ergo* someone killed him and we're back right where we started.'

They were silent and when he next spoke he did so very softly. 'Emma, what do you believe?'

She took her time. Both the scientist and the lawyer in her urged great caution.

'I have absolutely no evidence at all either way. The only fact I have is that your father did not die of a heart attack.

However, if you're asking me do I believe it is possible that your father was murdered, then I have to say "yes I do".'

'Right,' said Thierry determinedly, 'so let's go through that dossier again.'

He opened the file.

Though not large the dossier was very comprehensive and ordered. Official documents – minutes, memos, contracts and bank statements – were interleaved with notes in Marais' spidery handwriting. Shortly after he had arrived in Brussels, he received a call from the Financial Controller of DG VI – a Dutch woman – requesting a meeting. He, of course, had agreed but when she called something in her voice alerted him, so this had taken place not in his own office where one of his *cabinet* members would be in attendance, but at home.

His notes also recorded that she was well regarded as efficient and honest. She had taken up her post at a time of change – shortly after each Directorate had been made responsible for conducting their own audits and in-vestigating irregularities. Someone on the staff became suspicious of a superior. Gossip passed this suspicion on to her office and at first, gossip was all she had.

Nevertheless, she ordered a review of the contracts – how they had been awarded, to whom, where the money had gone and whether it had been accounted for. Soon she found a pattern of systematic irregularities that took three forms.

First, people and companies were being given privileged information about forthcoming contracts and direct help in winning them. Someone was monitoring the contracts on offer, then systematically lobbying staff members. One on whom pressure was being consistently applied was an Italian whose name had regularly cropped up earlier, in investigations going back as far as Quatraro.

But, equally compromising discrepancies were found at the other end of the process, when expenditures were audited. Once again the Financial Controller had asked two of her staff to review the details. They had found that bank statements, carelessly included in the files, were at variance with those formally presented in the audited accounts, and money which should have gone to one particular contractor could be seen to have ended up with another.

At this point Emma turned to Thierry and smiled.

He nodded in agreement. 'She was finding patterns.'

'Yes.'

These scams were not only pervasive in extent, but in substance too, covering a heap of products such as tobacco entering the Community duty free at one point for supposed export to Russia, but being systematically diverted to EU countries. There were transit frauds: goods came in from countries outside the Union and since they were destined for Middle Eastern countries and North Africa, via ships sailing from Marseilles and Lisbon, no duty was paid. Yet the goods never reached even these two ports, for shortly after their first entry point – generally the port of Amsterdam – the Customs seals were broken and the goods diverted to EU countries.

Emma was staggered, not so much by the huge sums involved, but the spider's web of connecting activity, cleverly controlled from just one point apparently.

'How on Earth did she find all this out?' she asked Thierry, as she handed him the pages.

'It's clear a few pages further on that UCLAF was finally told. Did you know about the country hot lines? I didn't.'

Some time later the Controller learnt that UCLAF had received anonymous calls on three country freephone lines – Denmark, Belgium and Britain. The ones from Denmark and Britain had given some details, but she didn't know whether contact numbers had been left. So, the existence of the calls apart, this was a dead end. But the Belgian call had come from a DG VI staff member – not Belgian – who had taken the opportunity to alert UCLAF. Whether this staff member was the original source of the internal gossip, she did not know. In any case, she now had strong evidence of systematic scams being run out of DG VI at the very highest level. And she had made it abundantly clear, that the 'highest level' included members of Marais' *cabinet*. However, she could give no further leads.

Marais' notes reveal that he took this last allegation very seriously, but immediately excluded his Musketeers, on the grounds that none had been in Brussels long enough to have got deeply involved and before that they had been safely tucked away in the Elysée Palace in Paris. It was at this point he made his visit to UCLAF and publicly asked for a meeting with an Investigating Magistrate.

'So that's why I saw him there,' murmured Emma.

'Yes,' said Thierry, 'but the meeting was singularly unsatisfactory.'

Marais' frustration was all over the notes. He first asked LeQuesne about UCLAF's procedures and then, had they any suspicions about DG staff members? If so, would he name them?

The answer was 'yes' to the first question, but an unequivocal 'no' to the second. When pressed LeQuesne had retreated behind a barrage of rationales: the need to preserve scrupulous fairness in UCLAF's investigations; for confidentiality – Marais was furious at any suggestion he would breach this; the obligation to acquire more evidence and investigate the motives of the whistle-blowers, and establish just where the criminal acts took place and just what, therefore, would be the legal basis for criminal investigation, by whom and where; the importance of these particular scams when weighed in the balance against other UCLAF investigations, and so on and so on and so on.

Marais revealed his frustration with a written comment: 'It will be just like the Quatraro affair: nothing will be done for years.'

But now he began to construct the third part of the dossier, conducting his own investigations, collecting documents from the office, noting his own suspicions and where the facts directed him. This was straight towards his *chef,* Felice Fede.

Armed with this knowledge he returned again to LeQuesne and asked him directly – did UCLAF harbour suspicions of Fede? Once again, LeQuesne had stonewalled and regretted but he was unable to reveal this information to Monsieur Le Commissaire. He was very sorry.

He wasn't sorry at all, Marais had noted. And that was that.

Emma got up, stretched and rubbed her eyes. Probably she needed spectacles. But damn it, she thought she'd got another few years at least. Thierry caught her look and smiled.

'I had to start wearing them last year,' he grinned.

'My God,' said Emma as she sat down again, 'your father must have spent hours and hours on this.'

'Yes,' said Thierry, 'but that's not the end. There's another paper I want you to see. It was locked away.' He opened a drawer in the right hand side of the desk and took out a single sheet – again written in Marais' spidery hand. This recorded the encounter with Dieter Bengt at the reception in the French Embassy and his possible blackmail. Then, with mounting horror, Emma read of the walk down the Chaussée de Waterloo and the car that with tyres screaming, nearly killed him.

She looked at Thierry and now she was white: 'Well, that's it isn't it?'

'Yes. I knew about this even while I was asking you whether you believed my father's death was not an accident. I am now convinced he was murdered.'

'Impossible, utterly impossible – in the sacred hall of Breydel during the President's lunch? No, not impossible. Where do we go from here?'

'Well, I'll see what I can get out of the Magistrate at UCLAF. His telephone number is in the file.'

'I'll have a chat with Céline Bardot. She's been here for years and years and knows far, far more than she's been saying.'

Thierry looked at his watch: 'Let's get together later. I'll pick you up at your hotel about seven o' clock and we'll have dinner?'

'That's a nice thought,' said Emma, making a mental note that he could do with a good meal, light conversation and an early night. But as things were going it was unlikely he'd get any of them.

CHAPTER FIFTEEN

The Silence of the Subsidies

Headline in *The European,* 6-12th January 1995

As Thierry entered LeQuesne's office in UCLAF, two young people promptly rose and left. Since the Magistrate appeared to have dropped everything, he hoped for a fruitful meeting.

He was to be disappointed. LeQuesne may have come from the Channel Isles – and that made him almost French – but he was most reluctant to discuss the Commissioner's concerns, even with his son.

Lanky and loose-limbed, with thin lips, a dry smile and receding hair, the Investigating Magistrate was Jacques Tati without any sense of the absurd. Thierry mistrusted him instinctively, which was surprising, for he took people at face value and most responded to his warm approach as they had to his father's.

After dancing around each other for a while in a polite ritual that was clearly leading nowhere, Thierry decided on a frontal attack.

'You will appreciate, Monsieur,' he said, 'my need to understand the circumstances. This was a terrible shock for our family.'

'I do indeed appreciate this,' murmured LeQuesne.

'So we are anxious to learn as much as possible. My father was a fit man who handled tension well. Thus I am looking for any unusual factors that might have precipitated this tragic event. Though it is true that he was still grieving over the death of my mother, he was not an obvious candidate for sudden cardiac arrest, unless of course, there were problems which he had kept hidden from everyone.'

'I appreciate that too,' murmured LeQuesne cautiously.

'Now, as his son it is my sad duty to settle his affairs. Yesterday I found a dossier in his desk that mentions certain matters he had discussed with you – concerning DG VI. Perhaps these were worrying him. Was my father involved in any crisis? I need your help.'

He watched Le Quesne's face intently. But the Magistrate rose, turned his back and restlessly fussed about for a moment. Then he went across to the window and leant on the radiator shelf, his back to the light. His face was in shadow, his expression hard to catch.

'There's no reason at all why I shouldn't be frank with you.'

Which means you are not going to be! Thierry was already angry.

'Your father's death has shocked us. Everyone in Brussels admired him greatly for his integrity. Neither a prevaricating politician nor a devious diplomat – and we get plenty of both here.'

Thierry acknowledged LeQuesne's words with a slight nod, but knew it was so much soft soap.

The Magistrate continued, 'First of all, let me make a general point. In discussions with my Commissioner, your father was told that UCLAF has never been given the necessary financial support or the personnel, to do its job properly. The nation states of the European Union are not as anxious to pursue crimes against the Community as they would have us believe. Thus much of the recent criticism directed against UCLAF is misplaced.'

'Is that so?'

'Criminals can commit fraud in one country, salt away goods in a second, the proceeds in a third and live in a fourth. Yet we have no power to question suspects, let alone arrest them; we are rarely given access even to the files, let alone the evidence. We can neither search premises nor seize documents, nor compel witnesses to come forward. We can request member states to carry out certain investigations, but we cannot insist. National imperatives override ours: political sensitivities always take precedent.'

'Is that all?' Thierry was not surprised but tried to restrain his sarcasm.

'No. Your father was different from many in the College. He disliked the hypocrisy involved and reacted angrily to fraud, especially when the possibility of redress was so circumscribed.'

'He was always like that,' said Thierry, now warming to the man. 'The stately, incestuous minuets of bureaucrats irritated him, especially when taken in conjunction with the omniscient way they treated the long-suffering taxpayers. The dossier I discovered in his desk is very comprehensive.'

'Did you bring it? We would very much like to see this.' LeQuesne sounded eager.

All Thierry's cautious instincts were aroused. I bet you would, but if flattery is all I'm going to get, you never will.

'I'm afraid I did not. But to return to my question. Could you tell me what was going on?'

'I cannot give you any information.'

'May I ask why?'

LeQuesne's eyes narrowed and Thierry knew there was more at stake than professional reticence – a double bluff, in fact. I want to know. But he wants to know how much Papa knew, before deciding whether to tell me anything. He's used to making other people reveal their hands.

'Monsieur, you should realise. Such matter as these are highly sensitive.'

'True, but fraud's been going on ever since the Community was first established. Surely we should take a stand?'

'Of course and we do. However, the real problem now is not so much that in monetary terms the amounts are great – though they are – but the degree of outside penetration. Organised crime is behind much of this. Mafia links are extensive, whether Italian, or Russian, or Albanian or whoever. The dimensions are now so large that in certain respects the situation has taken on the character of a war. It would be most unwise of me to reveal more.'

'So the Commission's courtly dances will continue even as the European Union's foundations are being undermined?'

LeQuesne endeavoured to look profoundly pained at both the emotive words and the implied slur.

'Monsieur, you cannot expect me to agree. Such matters take time and though the constraints on us are real, we proceed with our investigations conscientiously and swiftly. So what more can I tell you at this moment that would be helpful? Your father asked me certain questions; I responded as I felt appropriate.'

Inwardly Thierry was fuming. Papa was right – a good few years will now pass. So he rose to leave.

'And I too, am responding as I feel appropriate. I shall release my father's dossier when I see fit – to whom I will not say. Please contact me any time you wish. Thank you.'

But LeQuesne hesitated before opening the door.

'Monsieur, there is one thing more I told your father, that I believe you also should know.'

'Yes?'

'It can be dangerous to be interested in fraud in Brussels.'
'That is also in his files.'

Emma planned to slip into Breydel and see Arthos first. But she had a problem. Her *magnétique* had expired two days ago and though she was certain she could bamboozle her way into DG VI, it was highly unlikely she'd be successful in getting into Breydel. The guard's weapons were supposedly two machine-guns and some anti-tank weapons; hers mere deception. But there is no alternative, she told herself firmly.

So taking her passport, she returned to Breydel and at reception gave the name of a minor staff member – an efficient and effective Belgian lady – who had helped her sort out the files. Once on the phone Emma said: 'Anne-Marie, sorry to bother you, but could I come up for a moment, please? There's a couple of facts I need to check. I must produce an accurate copy of the report for my Board.'

Anne-Marie was most co-operative. She came down, retrieved Emma, and spent ten minutes chasing the errant facts. Then, just as Emma was trying to devise an excuse for making her own exit, the telephone rang.

Anne-Marie answered, 'Yes, of course. I'll be right over. Emma, can you find your own way out?' She spoke anxiously: the rules said she should escort her visitor down. But by now Emma was almost a permanent feature in the landscape.

'Of course,' said Emma brightly, not believing her luck. 'Don't worry at all,' and left.

Down the corridor, she turned right, walking with the confidence of familiarity. Another left turn along a smaller corridor. Still no one challenged her. She found his office and in response to her tap he said, *'Entrez'*.

There was no doubt Arthos was greatly surprised to see her. He jumped immediately to his feet, his face betraying that characteristic mixture of convincing deference, but not such convincing bravado, that Emma had often observed.

'Madame Austen,' he said with genuine puzzlement in his voice, 'I am delighted to see you but I understood you had returned to Cambridge?'

'No,' said Emma, slipping into the chair he offered. 'I had certain matters to complete after our meeting.'

'Well now, I'm not surprised.' He smiled. 'You exploded a few mines under us and though it wasn't my place to say so, I agreed with everything you said. We must resolve the beef mystery. Perhaps you have been taking this further with Dr Dashöfer? And the tobacco subsidies. Perhaps you have discussed these with Dr Fede? Governments can change as often as they like but lobbies remain.'

Remembering the not so solemn wink he had thrown her during the meeting, Emma was torn between laughter and severity. So she just ignored his sarcasm, then took a chance.

'Yesterday you denied that you had discussed fraud within DG VI with the Commissioner. That wasn't strictly true, was it?'

She smiled winsomely, one eyebrow raised and head slightly tilted sideways.

Arthos cheerfully returned her look and shook his head. 'No, it was not.'

'So why did you back down?'

'A number of reasons. I didn't want to give Sybilla any satisfaction at all.'

'Though when you backed down, surely you gave her a great deal?'

His head came up and he gave his characteristic shrug.

'Perhaps, but that was such a small victory I didn't really care. She doesn't like me, you know. She has the natural disdain of the aristocrat for the bourgeoisie. But that too, doesn't matter. However, she does hate being out of the loop. She wants to know everything – but everything – that is going on. And she was having an affair with the Commissioner.'

'There's always gossip.'

'You know it's true. This started soon after the Piedmont mission. The Commissioner was clearly very sad when he first arrived.'

'Did you mind?'

'Not my place to mind, one way or the other. I cared about the Commissioner's serenity though.'

'Did she give him that?'

'Reluctant though I am to admit it, she did – some – and she became a touch less imperious, too.'

'But you haven't answered my other question,' said Emma flatly.

'No I haven't,' he replied, equally flatly. 'Though I don't see any reason not to. The Commissioner had discussed the matter with me. A new directive had come through that made each Directorate responsible for investigating improprieties amongst their own staff. He took this very seriously indeed.

'Let's be quite clear. He was not inviting me to be Maigret, but he did instruct me to become *au fait* about earlier affairs and what – if anything – UCLAF presently suspected about fraud within DG VI. I was generally to enquire around and see what turned up. The Commissioner's contacts, of course, were with his opposite number and an examining Magistrate, LeQuesne. Mine were within the UCLAF *cabinet*.'

Emma made a guess. 'A beautiful blonde.'

Arthos was temporarily startled. 'Ah yes. You saw her escorting us out of the building. She's Finnish.'

How close are you now, Emma wondered.

'At first I wondered why me? Why not the *chef*, or other people who'd been around much longer. But then I figured the Commissioner knew I had no axe to grind and I was so new that I wouldn't have had enough time to get involved in whatever scams were going on – for all that I'm intelligent and energetic! And he also knew that though I'm very ambitious, I don't mind getting into political hot water.'

'But these two traits could cancel each other out,' observed Emma. 'The other day you admitted your wish to ascend the political ladder to the very highest rung. Wouldn't expediency rather than a scalding be a better strategy?'

'Did you say scolding?'

'No, scalding – but the effect would be the same.'

'Well, there is more than one way to ascend. The smooth diplomatic approach, when expediency rules is one. But sheer, dominating brilliance is another.'

He grinned and Emma could not help responding to the young monkey. What would be his ultimate fate? Falling flat on his face, or shooting upwards like a rocket? Probably the latter, for he was more than a natural survivor. He intended to dictate the terms of his life and no matter how vicious the political rough and tumble, would always land on his feet.

She hesitated a moment, wondering whether to question him further.

'Then just what did you discover about fraud within DG VI?'

'Very little.'

As he had two days earlier, he now became absolutely still and as then, so now, she knew he was lying. Still, she hesitated. It wasn't that pressure would be inappropriate at this moment – he could cope with that – so much as counter-productive.

'Did you ever wish you were an *énarque*?' she asked.

'No fear,' he replied. 'Especially not now. Can you believe it, applications to our venerable Academy dropped by a full third this year.'

'Now there's a surprise!' She laughed and rose.

He shot to his feet and with practised courtesy opened the door.

'I have to call on Céline Bardot,' she said.

'Then let me escort you to the elevator,' he said. 'You will notice that I'm not asking you why.'

'I wouldn't have told you.'

They walked amicably together to the lobby. One elevator arrived immediately but as Emma moved to enter, Sybilla Høgstrøm emerged and caught her by the arm.

'My dear Emma, I'm astonished. How delightfully unexpected. How much longer are you staying in Brussels? Let us have lunch together or, best of all, come and have dinner. When are you free?'

'I'm not sure,' replied Emma deliberately vague, 'But yes, I'd love to.'

'We have so much to settle,' Sybilla continued regally. 'The Commissioner's son was in for a brief meeting with Dr Fede. What a charming young man; what a terrible tragedy for the family. Emma,' she went on, 'we are so grateful to you for realising that Thierry would arrive in Brussels not knowing the dreadful news. I'm ashamed that none of us thought of this.'

'You don't need to feel ashamed,' said Emma. 'At such moments everyone is trying to keep on an even keel. It was one small, practical thing I could do.'

'But nevertheless we are most grateful,' repeated Sybilla. 'Emma,' she continued, her tone imperious now, 'I insist you do not leave Brussels without seeing me again.'

During this exchange Emma noticed that Sybilla had ignored Arthos completely. As she sailed serenely off, Emma turned, shook his hand, then caught the next elevator down one floor.

Céline Bardot carefully steered the conversation away from Marais' death. In fact she steered Emma out of the building to a local coffee-house, as if Emma no longer belonged. Emma was glad: she didn't want to linger in Breydel. She tried to dispel their earlier coolness and let the talk range where it would. But finally it was Céline who opened up.

'Such sad and difficult times,' she observed. 'Very hard – no time to think, no time to reflect. But that's been our problem for years – quite unlike when I first started here. There's so much to do now with so many briefing papers to prepare, in so many languages. We never catch up. And I find it very difficult to accommodate myself to the new thinking that pervades the House these days.'

'What new thinking?' Emma prodded.

'Well, the idealism has gone.'

'You think so?'

'Oh, yes. I'm not certain why this happened. It's more than just the invasion of infantile, political careerists who do not share the vision, or the fact that we are all so over-worked that we have lost sight of the fundamentals. Whatever the reason, it's a tragedy.'

'That's a very emotive word. You really believe the vision has vanished?'

'I don't want to believe so. This would be a betrayal of everything I've ever worked for in all my years here. We had a dream and it was one that could be realised. A political union, with ties so firm and efforts directed to such worthy causes that there *could* be no more wars – only universal justice and true social equality.'

'There's a real problem with visions,' observed Emma drily, 'they have a horrible habit of colliding with the irritating facts of everyday life.'

'How cynical you are.'

'Not at all – just realistic.'

Céline paused while the waitress served the coffee. 'I must admit I like you British,' she finally observed. 'Though for the life of me I don't know why, for I will never understand you. Many of us in Brussels will never understand you.'

'Who is "us"?' queried Emma. 'Those present at the Creation...?'

'There you go again,' said Céline, 'always facetious. Take the Social Chapter or the Commission's new Charter of Rights. How can you British *not* accept what we propose? How could you not believe in the betterment of fellow humans?'

'It's not that we don't believe in it, but we are very realistic about the price to be paid.'

'What does the price matter? None can be too great, no burden too heavy, to achieve universal social justice.'

Oh, for God's sake, thought Emma with sudden, irritated impatience, cut it out. Who does she think she is? Karl Marx; a candidate for Presidency of the USA? I'm sure she's really a good person but she should come down off Cloud Nine and live in the real world.

'The price does matter.'

'What could we expect from a nation of shopkeepers?' said Céline with sad resignation, brushing the hair back from her face. 'We must never forget that Margaret Thatcher was a grocer's daughter.'

'And what's wrong with that?' asked Emma sharply.

'Nothing, except that grocers are not famous for their vision.'

'But they are for their practical common sense.'

'But what can that achieve of itself?' argued Céline. Then she hesitated so long that Emma thought she was about to suggest they leave. Duty surely called loudly from the towers of Breydel. But Céline was in no hurry and when finally she spoke it was in a tone of conciliation mixed with reluctant admiration.

'Though I'll tell you something else, Emma, something everyone in the House agrees with. You British may be difficult – you may be troublesome...'

'Along with the Danes,' insisted Emma, as she had done earlier to Marais. Damned if she was going to be isolated.

'Indeed, the Awkward Squad. You may, as we believe, be stolid, insular and very limited in your approach. But if we want anyone to present a case, write a document, participate in a meeting, then no one – but no one – comes better prepared. The background briefing of your people is so comprehensive. Every aspect of a problem is studied, not a single detail missed. I've said this publicly and I'll say it to you. I would rather have someone British working alongside me than anyone else.'

'Well, thank you very much indeed,' smiled Emma with a hint of sarcasm. 'How fascinating to see our different national styles being revealed in politics. I'm used to it in the way we do science – which can bring astonished cries from our more theoretical French colleagues. But I've never before heard it applied to a bureaucracy. You really see the Union as a vision, don't you, rather than an evolving process?' she asked.

'I'm not that hidebound,' protested Céline. 'Of course, we have to evolve. You know,' she went on quietly. 'Over the years I've seen them all come and go. You must believe me, Emma,' she was almost pleading, 'there are many, many wonderful people around – amongst the Commissioners, the permanent staff, the Council of Ministers – who work enormously hard and do a fantastic job.'

'I'm sure there are.'

'So people who believe the Commission is rotten at the core are plain wrong. True: there are some holding high office who are totally worthless and for whom we have great contempt. But they provide another reason why I believe that those of us who have the vision must direct progress.'

Now Emma felt more than a twinge of impatience. This was just too much.

'On behalf of the rest of us?'

'On behalf of the rest. So though I am reluctant to say this, I think the Commissioner was quite wrong, God rest his soul. I saw what he was trying to do, but I truly believe it was unnecessary.'

'Hmm,' Emma commented: 'Thy Kingdom come, on bended knee we pray.'

'Ah no – not just that,' said Céline with a terrible, humourless sincerity. 'We don't remain on bended knee. We get up and fight for the Kingdom that is yet to come.'

Emma changed the subject. She hadn't come to participate in a revival meeting.

'The other day Arthos was talking about the Commissioner's concern about fraud. And Sybilla sat on him.'

'I should have sat on him,' said Céline, 'but Sybilla got there first. She usually does. Of course, we know there have been some external problems with the agricultural subsidies. But are people within the Directorate actively involved in internal frauds and criminal activities? No, I insist: I don't believe so. The Quatraro case was a one-off.'

But her hand was nowhere near the recalcitrant locks: it had stopped just by her mouth.

Emma regarded her sceptically. I haven't mentioned internally directed fraud, she thought, so why did you? And what were you doing with those files that night? Oh hell, on the face of it, you're such a good person, with that gentle open face. But then again, you could be hiding something, disappearing into the silence of the subsidies.

She signalled the waitress and called for the bill.

As they walked from the restaurant, Céline nervously retreated into herself. But when she finally spoke Emma knew she really did have something to hide.

'I'm going to resign.'

CHAPTER SIXTEEN

Out of the Cul-de-Sac

Mankind always sets itself only such problems as it can solve;
since, looking at the matter more closely, it will always be found that the task
itself arises only when the material conditions for its solution already exist or
are at least in the process of formation.

Karl Marx: Preface, *A Critique of Political Economy*

In spite of Emma's good intentions the evening was a disaster. They inevitably returned to the distressing topic and Thierry looked utterly defeated.

'It's hopeless. We are no nearer knowing why my father died.'

'No, it's not.' But she could not even convince herself.

He pushed his plate away and sighed. 'I'll give it another day. Then I must take him home and try to pick up the threads of my life. Forgive me.'

'But, of course,' said Emma, as they rose. What else could she say? She too, had another life – somewhere.

Back at the hotel she felt deflated, carrying the burden of Thierry's defeatism at a time when she wanted to feel optimistic. But in truth her soul was in emotional turmoil – grief battling with a puzzling challenge; the mystery battling with rapidly developing feelings for a very personable young man.

She was also very tired – too tired even to weep – not certain why the finality of Thierry's last words had so upset her, though surely it was because they marked the end of her connections with Charles Marais and his son.

She flung herself on the bed. What really was her interest in all this? An intellectual mystery, that the scientific detective wanted to unravel? Or had Thierry's father been right and they could make each other happy? And how, for God's sake, she told herself furiously, could she possibly answer that question at this moment.

What had begun as a simple job for Components, to be neatly completed in a finite period, had metamorphosed into a deadly game, where rationality was undermined by suspicion, logic with pain. How naïve she'd been when she had booked that ticket to Brussels, confident that she would not have to make any personal choices, let alone difficult ones.

But the time had come when she must either face again the pains of life or live with the fact that she was a coward. However wounding those earlier defeats, encouraging the growth of emotional scar tissue had been a mistake. So now deliberately, she recalled her past.

A scientist by training, Emma was soon forced to realise that she would never be a successful one. This unpleasant truth had arrived too late for peace of mind, for she was well into post-doctoral research in San Francisco and a deep love affair with an American colleague, when she had to admit that everything was going horribly wrong.

In truth she was a scientist *manqué*. While the ideas of science enthralled her, the laboratory stifled her. As the poet said, she constantly 'heard the afternoon sun knocking', but rather than 'loving the white coated sterility' of the laboratory, she hated it. For Emma possessed only fifty per cent of the skills every good scientist needs.

Creative imagination she had in plenty, and could apply self-criticism to her own ideas and match the best and the most rigorous of her colleagues as she did so. But other aspects defeated her. Laboratory routines – testing and retesting, designing experiments, ironing out the technical problems, not once but over and over again – became a stifling strait-jacket.

The end finally came in the simplest of ways, a defining moment on a truly disastrous day. First of all, she received irrefutable evidence that her lover – a brilliant but arrogant scientist had blithely appropriated not only her body, but her experimental results too. Emma resented the theft of the science very much, but that of her self-esteem even more. Then at work, her experiments wouldn't work, the samples were contaminated, the power to the deep-freeze went off, the backup too, failed, and such results as she finally managed to produce were irritatingly ambiguous. To crown it all she dropped a bottle of reagents on the laboratory floor. The silly, small accident of shattered glass became the symbol. Life couldn't go on like this. She was furious not only with him, but even more with herself. In truth, her wounds were self-inflicted. Stupid not to have seen the devastating consequences of both mistakes – job and heart – looming ahead.

Her decision – the wisest she had ever made – was immediate and she never looked back. She quit the laboratory, her love affair and California in that order. Once back in Britain, she used a legacy from her parents to study law and set out to rediscover Europe and herself.

She sailed through the examinations, then was lucky enough to be taken on for the required two years' practical experience, by a law firm in St James's Square, London, that specialised in media. A full-blown solicitor, by chance she met up with Jane again who was looking for something to do. Together they decided to try their luck and founded Components.

Now years later, here she was in Brussels and Euroland – with all that this implied. But I don't belong here, she thought. I am amongst strangers.

Propped on the pillows, she took a cold look at the hotel bedroom and knew that she'd had just about enough. She hated its faded red carpet and the patterned counterpane of the bed; irritated by the small bedside lamps that had less light than a single firefly, and the plastic fittings.

Suddenly she knew what she wanted – the chime of the bells, the colour of Jesus Green, the familiar routines of the office, Jane's calm presence and Ned's joking conversation. She wanted her own house in New Square, to feel the rugs under her bare feet, to smell the roses on the wall and even chase the trespassing cats from the garden. She said aloud: 'I want to go home.'

But because she sounded so like a small child, she began to laugh. Then, just as suddenly as a small child she began to weep. But her tears were those of an adult who comprehends the dark, finality of death.

Twenty-four hours later she was back in Cambridge. Before leaving she had called Thierry but the maid had said '*Je regrette, mais Monsieur est sorti.*'

Jane had long been in when Emma finally arrived at the office. She had taken her time, revelling in the peaceful familiarity of her house, checking its boundaries for reassurance. She had been on a very long journey. The evening before she had sat quietly in a sitting-room that reflected her personality well. There were a few antiques that had come to her through the family – an eighteenth-century walnut bureau against one wall; a small Georgian footpad table served as her dining table; four watercolours on the wall, depicting scenes from the Lake District and the Alps, painted by Howard Somervell – who was with Mallory and Irving on Everest. The garden held one rose still, but no signs of a single trespassing cat. Her serenity would quickly return.

Next day she walked happily to the office in the small house at the top of Portugal Place, between the calm of Jesus Green and the scurrying humanity of Bridge Street. Yet traces of the stress and fatigue must have lingered on her face for Jane looked up and said, 'You're glad to be back.'

'Very,' said Emma, and moved forward to give her a big hug.

'Tell me everything when you're ready.' Jane understood her Emma and was not about to press. She guessed the events of the last forty-eight hours must have been harrowing. But Emma had told her nothing about Thierry and even though, two days later, she spent another cheerful evening out at Elmdon, she stayed silent about him and their joint suspicions about Marais' death.

In any case, she was soon to be fully occupied. Another job had come in from Brussels, this time from DG XII, Science and Research. Emma decided to hand over that to one of her brilliant graduates. A television production company had requested their consulting skills on yet another film on the BSE crisis. She handed on that one, too. The Director of a new charity asked for a meeting to discuss a conference on whither, scientifically, the world was going and what should be done about it. If I only knew, sighed Emma, still flat and tired. An entry in her diary reminded her that, in a few days' time, she had to be at the Dorchester Hotel, London, for the annual Science Writers Awards, sponsored by a British pharmaceutical company. As Chairperson of the Awards Committee she would be expected to make a splendid speech after a splendid dinner. I hate being a 'Chairperson', she thought – so neutered!

Life quickly resumed its familiar rhythms, but try as she might, the puzzle of Marais' death would not leave her, troubling her sub-conscious and niggling her intellect. Memories of Thierry and his 'There's something not quite right' wove into her dreams.

She knew something was badly wrong.

On a whim she telephoned her friend in Paris, Annette Gellibert des Seguins, a distinguished art historian. Please could she send a postcard of the Fra Angelico painting? Three days later this arrived along with a two-page interpretation of the poignant female faces, that included the same comment made by Thierry: 'One of the saints in blue is possibly St Mary Magdalene, but she is holding her head too high.'

Emma rang to ask why her mien raised questions of identity. Because, Annette said, she was supposed to be a prostitute and traditional representations always portrayed her in a suitably humble pose. However, anyone invited to the coronation of the Virgin Mary could surely be excused a little pride!

Then one week later, securely settled into routine and Cambridge, her tranquillity was disturbed again. Arthos called from Paris, ostensibly to see how she was. But he sounded anxious, as if he needed to talk.

'Why are you in Paris, not Brussels?' enquired Emma, inquisitive as ever.

Arthos was frank. 'I have been recalled. The official line is because the whole *cabinet* will soon change. But I've been under pressure from Dr Fede. He didn't quite tell me to shove off, but did indicate that my activities were now surplus to requirements!'

'His or DG VI's?' queried Emma.

'He put it in terms of the Directorate's of course, but I think they're his. He's anxious to consolidate his position before Senor Prodi arrives. He wants to stay. But, Madame Austen, there's something else. Could I see you?'

'Well...' said Emma vaguely. 'Not in the immediate future. We've a full workload and I'm in the throes of writing a speech for an awards ceremony this week. Is there anything particular on your mind?'

'Yes,' he replied promptly. 'First of all, I am horribly lonely. My Finnish goddess – '

'Your what...?'

'Didn't I tell you? I'm sure I did. My stunning girlfriend in the UCLAF *cabinet* – and we were getting along so well. But I'm now back in Paris and she is off on a mission somewhere obscure, I think, like Bosnia or Bulgaria. No, it's Andorra.'

'Why there?'

'Problems with tobacco fraud. The Andorrans swear they don't smuggle cigarettes but they do.'

Damn, thought Emma, here we go again.

'Do they?'

'And how. In the last four years cigarette imports into Andorra shot up a hundred fold. They claim they're used there. In that case one million Andorrans somehow manage to smoke nine million a day! A clear case for UCLAF – not to mention cancer specialists. So, you see, I'm abandoned – a free agent.'

Emma still hesitated. Just what was he hoping for?

'Seriously though, do you remember our last conversation? Please, Madame Austen, you must listen. I have uncovered some information that the Commissioner would have liked to have known.'

'What kind of information? Why is this important now?'

His voice lost all its levity.

'I'd rather not talk about this over the phone if you don't mind.'

Yet for the third time Emma hesitated. If he really had new information she wanted Thierry to be present. But just where was Thierry? He'd not been in touch. Did Arthos too, harbour suspicions about Marais' death? Or did he just want to unburden his lovesick soul to a third party?

But with as much warmth as she could muster – for she was fighting to protect her tranquillity – she asked for his telephone number and promised to be in touch once the workload eased. But she didn't really know whether she would.

But Brussels and Marais were not so easily banished. Between decisions and writing and discussions and relaxation – she adored *Shakespeare in Love* – she toyed with the idea of ringing Thierry. But she knew that other than wanting to hear his voice, she had neither reason nor pretext and could not begin to guess his reactions. True: she had warmed to him during those days but had he become really important? As she kept prevaricating the intellectual puzzle continued to taunt her: she hated loose ends and she hated not knowing.

Another forty-eight hours were to pass before events made up her mind. 'It was on a Monday morning', so the old song went, and it *was* on a Monday morning. She always took the first hour of each day at a deliberately slow pace. This meant going downstairs and making a large mug of tea. While waiting for the kettle to boil she would stroll to the window, gaze into the garden, retrieve *The Times* from the doormat and return to bed, skimming the headlines first then reading any articles.

That morning the mug was on the bedside table and she was slowly turning the pages, when an advertisement caught her eye. Placed by Sainsbury's, it was a warning – a batch of yoghurt whose contents had been incorrectly labelled and customers were advised to return their purchases at once.

Emma read the advertisement three times – very slowly. Then suddenly she sat up, moving so fast that she hit the mug. The tea spilt down *The Times* and over the sheets. She swore softly, then futilely started to mop at both, as her thoughts raced and she struggled to complete the connections her mind had offered.

A Fra Angelico painting from Tuscany, a liqueur, Frangelica, from Piedmont, a Sainsbury's advertisement – all three kept spinning around – so rapidly that she didn't quite know what to do next. Her head was throbbing with echoes. A fresh copy of *The Times* could be bought, the sheets were due to be changed anyway. For it was Monday, the traditional washday – or was that just the day the gasman came to call?

She showered, dressed, had a quick breakfast while waiting impatiently for the shops to open. She needed to set all the pieces physically in front of her eyes, not just logically in her mind. But as she went through her familiar routine, one irritating – even humiliating – bubble of thought slowly began making its way up through every other notion occupying her brain. What an absolute fool she had been.

She had to visit three off-licences in all. Eaden Lilley, near the Market Place, and en route to her office, was her first port of call. Surely their exotic liqueur section, next to their delicatessen, would carry it? But no. Polite though they were, she got the impression they considered it a sweet drink for the proletarian masses.

So she crossed Market Place, swung right and made her way to Oddbins in Bridge Street. They were extremely helpful, but again she drew a blank.

'Well, we know it of course, but it's much more popular in the States. But we could easily get it for you.'

Emma was beginning to think she would have to go to London and try all the Italian shops in Soho. But with Bottoms Up, also in Bridge Street, she hit pay dirt.

'You're in luck,' the assistant said cheerfully. 'I know we've got a couple of bottles at the back,' and went to get one. 'Don't sell many of these,' he said as he wrapped it up.

Emma thanked him with such effusive gratitude that the assistant, who was small and had never made it with any of the girls, began to think his luck was about to change.

Armed with briefcase, bottle and Sainsbury's ad, Emma walked round the corner to Portugal Place to find Jane already working.

'Shopping for something special?' she enquired, looking at the bag.

'I'm not really sure.' Emma looked so preoccupied that Jane, used to her introspective moods, said nothing.

Once in her office, Emma went to her desk and pushed aside the waiting files. Then she placed the three objects in line – to her left the postcard of the Fra Angelico painting; in the centre, the bottle of Frangelica, the specialist liqueur from Piedmont, courtesy of Bottoms Up; on her right, the Sainsbury's advertisement from the morning's *Times*. As her gaze moved from one to the next to the next, and back again to the first, she heard Marais' voice. 'Don't ever muddle up anything with Fra Angelico. I'm a devoted fan.' Then her own – asking Thierry: 'What did he find appealing about Fra Angelico's work?'

Thierry's voice: 'People spoke of him as a man of simplicity and saintly temperament, who led a calm, quiet life. I suppose the one element in him that did converge with Fra Angelico was his sense of tranquil acceptance.'

Finally, she read the label on the bottle of the liqueur:

According to the legend Fra Angelico lived three centuries ago in the hilly area bound by the right bank of the River Po. He lived as a hermit and through his love of nature and knowledge of its secrets created unique recipes for liqueurs.

The most precious one of all was a liqueur created from wild hazelnuts and infusions of berries and flowers to enrich the flavor. We continue the tradition by proudly offering this fine liqueur in honor of his name.

Produced by the Barbero Family.
Barbero S.P.A. Canale, Italy

Three men – three, essentially simple men. All now dead. One perhaps, had never lived. But centuries ago someone had stumbled upon a secret to make the liqueur, which posterity and clever marketing, had endowed with the mystique of a hermit living in tune with nature.

The Dominican monk, also a painter, equally in harmony with his world, whose belief in God, the Divine Creator, was reflected in paintings that touched eternity.

And Marais. Who was Marais? What would be Marais' legacy?

For a few minutes longer she sat quite passively, just letting her mind range where it would. Many years ago in New York a distinguished neuro-pharmacologist told her that every time he felt trapped in an intellectual cul-de-sac, facing a problem that he could not resolve, he would – as he went to bed – say firmly to his mind, 'Subconscious, take care of this.' And it was amazing how many times he awoke in the morning with the problem either solved, or the direction he should take crystal-clear.

Again Emma laughed ruefully and said again: 'How very stupid of me,' and went into the adjoining room.

'Jane,' she said, 'Could you please help me?'

'Of course.'

'I need to reach Dr Thierry Marais urgently. If I try his flat in Paris and the house in Brussels, could you try the company headquarters?'

She drew a blank, but fifteen minutes later a triumphant Jane came into Emma's office. 'Got him! He's in a meeting but his assistant has promised faithfully to give him the message the moment he's out.'

'Did she say when it would finish?' asked Emma impatiently.

'No, she didn't and why don't you just tell me what's on your mind?'

As she waited – for two long hours it turned out – she tried to curb her impatience, as quietly she told Jane everything that had happened during her last days in Brussels. Jane asked all the right questions and none of the invasive ones. Emma was grateful. She didn't want anyone urging her to examine her feelings right now. They could – yet again – be conveniently shoved to one side while the intellectual puzzle was tackled.

But feelings were not totally banished.

'You know me, Jane. Once I know how to solve a problem I just rush straight ahead and solve it. But I've got to be very careful with Thierry. He's just buried his father and...'

'He'll be feeling raw.'

'...and might just want to forget the whole business.'

Precisely at noon the call came through.

CHAPTER SEVENTEEN

The Process of Formation

By, heaven, he echoes me,
As if there were some monster in his thoughts
Too hideous to be shown.

Shakespeare: *Othello*

There was no mistaking the pleasure in his voice.

'Emma, what a lovely surprise. I've been thinking so much about you. How are you?'

'Very well, thank you.'

But he detected a note of anxiety.

'Emma, are you all right? What's wrong?'

'I'm not certain how to put this, Thierry, but I think I know why your father died.'

'You do? How do you know?'

'Well, to be truthful, actually I don't. There's something I need to check first and I don't want to raise false hopes.'

'What's involved?'

'A simple test. I need a blood sample sent to the University of Southampton. Robert Dewiere will have one.'

'He certainly will. You remember our last discussion?'

How could she forget?

'Well, I rang and said I wasn't satisfied and expected all blood and tissue samples to be retained. I wasn't at all popular.'

'Good for you. But I didn't know what you'd be feeling – whether you'd want to keep this enquiry going.'

He hesitated for a long moment. More turmoil, no guarantee of success.

'Emma, how sure are you?'

Now she hesitated.

'Well, I'm confident I'm on the right track. But if my hunch turns out to be wrong, then I'll not only be totally baffled but also deeply sorry for bringing this up. But the blood-test will tell us.'

'All right, how soon would you like it?'

'The quicker the better.'

'Let me make a couple of phone calls and I'll get right back to you.'

'Are you sure?... I don't want...'

'Don't worry. I'm quite sure.'

Ten minutes later he was back.

'I've spoken to Dewiere. I'll send the company plane to Brussels and the sample can be flown to Southampton whenever you wish. So, where will you be?'

'Can you hang on a minute, Thierry.' She grabbed her diary and flipped through the entries of the next two days.

'Look, I'd like to be there when they do the test. I have to go to London this afternoon for a bash at the Dorchester. But I can get down to Southampton first thing in the morning. In fact, I could meet the plane at Eastleigh Airport and take the sample straight over.'

'Suppose I give instructions that the pilot is to be at Eastleigh around 10.30 a.m. or so, is that okay?'

'That's fine. Thank you.'

'And then what?'

'Well, if it tells us what I think it's going to tell us, then I shall have to go back to Brussels.'

'In that case I'll come too. How long will the test take?'

'Oh – if they get the sample by 11 a.m., I'll know by the evening.'

'Then, Emma, why don't you spend a second night in Southampton? The plane can either wait at Eastleigh if no one else needs it, or come back for you early in the morning, fly you to Brussels and I'll join you there.'

'I was hoping you would,' murmured Emma. 'But where can I reach you? If the whole thing turns out to be a dead duck there'll be no need for either of us to go to Brussels.'

'True. However, dead duck or no dead duck, I want to see you again. So, in that case how about a few days in Paris?'

Emma smiled – delicious tempation. 'Let's see,' she offered cautiously. 'Thierry?'

'Yes?'

'What's the French equivalent of dead duck? It can't be *canard mort*, and the only other thing I can think of is *canard en presse*.'

He laughed. 'Both wrong. *Canard boiteux* is what you want. Not dead, but lame – one leg shorter than the other!'

Still smiling, Emma put the phone down, then spent the next half hour with Jane discussing work and collecting her passport, Eurocheques and currency out of the office safe. Back at New Square she watered the plants and packed for three nights, choosing her clothes and scarves carefully. Thierry must know thousands of elegant French women.

Then suddenly she remembered Arthos' call. Had he really found out something important? There was only one way to find out. So she rang and said she might well be in Brussels, or Paris, during the next few days.

'I'm so pleased. Where, when, would you like to meet?' said Arthos eagerly.

'Can I let you know later? I'll be with Thierry Marais.'

She sensed the disappointment in his reply, but yes, he would be around.

A taxi to the station, the Cambridge Flyer to King's Cross and within two hours she was ensconced in a suite in the Dorchester which, as Chairman of the Awards Committee, she had been allocated by the sponsoring company. Equivalent to at least four rooms of her Brussels hotel, Emma frankly revelled in the luxury. Quickly unpacking, she decided to go the whole hog, so called room service and ordered China tea and cucumber sandwiches. Kicking off her shoes, she danced over the carpet, toes gently massaged by the thick pile.

I'm a sybarite at heart, she told herself. Though this was not totally true she was happy to indulge after the strains of the last week. But the puritan soon emerged and with the tea by her side, she firmly parked herself down at the desk and reviewed her speech.

That done, the sybarite again drove out the puritan. She ran a hot bath, threw into it all the most deliciously scented things she could find and lay back. Every part of her slim body disappeared beneath the bubbles, except her toes,which were fiddling with the taps and her head which rested on a towel. She looked at what she could see of herself in the mirror, and thought – a glass of champagne, please. Then send for the photographers.

She took her time but once wrapped in the largest bath towel she had ever seen, she couldn't help making quantitative comparison again. One Dorchester towel equals six times a Brussels one. As she dried and applied cologne, she remembered she was about to be flown to Brussels in a private plane, and she laughed aloud. I could get used to this.

At half past six, she went down to the gilded foyer as other members of the Award Committee were drifting in, to meet with the Chairman of the pharmaceutical company. They had enjoyed their earlier sessions together and since their final meeting was uncontentious, Emma had little to do. None of them, she noticed, had stumbled into a 'person hole' on the way to the meeting and none of them called her 'Madam Chair', or anything except 'Emma'. They confirmed their unanimous decisions over the award winners and the points that they wanted her to raise in her speech, on the problems of scientific communication at the end of the Millennium.

At a quarter past seven they moved into the Orchard Room, decorated in a blue and white Wedgwood motif that Emma found more than acceptable, topped by a six foot chandelier that she regarded warily. Gradually some ninety people came in for dinner at ten circular tables and the ceremony began.

Such occasions can be truly ghastly, but Emma enjoyed the whole evening. The event was important but not momentous, so there was an intimacy about the proceedings and naturally the food and wine were delicious. She enjoyed her fellow guests – on her right, the Company Chairman, a bluff dynamic Yorkshireman; on her left, David Collins, the President of the British Association of Science Writers, a journalist she had known for years. Her speech was well received by the audience of the company's invited guests and journalists and television or radio producers. She laced congratulations with anecdotes, added a warning about smugness and the need to strike a balance between sticking to well-tried formulae and becoming anarchic in the search for originality. Finally, she rejoiced in the procession of bright young people who now came forward to receive their awards.

The Chairman briskly congratulated everyone in sight, thanked the Committee for their six months' hard labour, closed the proceedings and left. But David suggested a nightcap and Emma, feeling exhilarated and very wide awake, was happy to agree.

He knew his way to the bar instinctively, as good journalists always do, and steered her across the foyer towards the Park Lane side of the hotel. Two people, possibly three, could just walk side by side along the narrow corridor into the bar, so anyone wanting a private drink with their lover is advised to take a room. It is not possible to avoid being seen – just as Céline Bardot and Sir Robert Partridge could not avoid seeing Emma as they emerged.

In the split second before she was recognised, Emma noticed that Partridge's hand was on the nape of Céline's neck. Céline, looking relieved and tranquil, seemed triumphant.

Emma's mind raced. This can't be because he's seduced her. She can't be that desperate; she has more taste. And why is he looking so pleased with himself?

Partridge momentarily relinquished his hold on Céline and said smugly, 'Good evening, Emma,' as casually as if they were in the Combination Room of St Peter's. Then he moved on, pulling at Céline a little.

But she freed herself and turned back.

'Emma, what on Earth are you doing here?'

'Attending an awards ceremony,' replied Emma, a grinning David standing by her side, regarding the scene with lively interest. 'And you? I didn't know you knew Sir Robert.'

'Oh, I met him many years ago, when I first began in Brussels.'

Ah, yes, Emma thought...those present at the Creation.

Céline was clearly flustered and seemed anxious to explain, but a few paces away, Partridge had turned back, impatient, and, Emma thought, angry.

Céline's hand went up to her mouth: 'I've been discussing with him what I shall do when I retire.'

A lie, thought Emma. 'You will write your memoirs, perhaps?'

'There you go again,' said Céline, shaking her head in disapproval, 'always facetious. No, he's most interested in all the developments in Brussels.'

Now that possibly is true.

'You remember I told you I was resigning. I wanted to discuss matters with Sir Robert and he's been giving me most valuable advice.'

Another lie. Partridge's advice would be totally self-serving.

'Emma, it's so nice to see you again.'

Oh dear, yet another lie.

'Have a nice evening,' Céline concluded.

Now this really is a time to be curious, Emma decided. Why was she so uncomfortable? What was she doing here? – and followed David down the steps and left into the ornate and famous bar.

Tall, with ginger hair and running to fat, David chain-smoked which Emma found trying. But he was a superb science writer and she liked him. He eased his way into a comfortable chair, caught the waiter's eye immediately - a successful gesture polished by years of practice. Emma studied the panels on the wall and their ornate motifs. Birds of paradise, were they? – some on perches, eyeing butterflies and dragon flies – others in cages. How fitting. Céline was giving every appearance of being caged.

David raised his glass to her.

'Now what was all that about?'

'I rather wish I knew.'

'But you'll undoubtedly find out,' said David. 'I've rarely met anyone as inquisitive as you, Emma. Sorry, I'm making that sound a little too pejorative. But you have a very restless mind.'

'I should hope so. And I've noticed that you have one too.'

'Can get one into a whole heap of trouble,' said David. 'But then I've a wife and kids to fall back on. You know, Emma, we all care a great deal about you.' Her background was common knowledge. 'Is everything going okay?'

'That's sweet of you, David. Yes, it is,' she said in a tone of uncertainty which he spotted.

'Well, I'm glad. But don't try to be too secure.'

'You're not talking about my profession, are you?' she said.

'You know damn well I'm not. I'm talking about your love life.'

Between David's final remark and the puzzle of Céline's presence, Emma didn't get off to sleep for a couple of hours, for all that the bed was as comfortable as any demanding sybarite could desire and a puritan disapprove – pure Irish linen sheets and all.

She'd first encountered Roger Scaife at a conference. Now they met in the main entrance hall of a hospital – standing on their own private island amongst a sea of anxious relatives, determined doctors, preoccupied nurses. Though a Lecturer in Immunopharmacology in the Department of Medicine at the University, Roger was based in the General Hospital in Southampton. She handed over the package she had earlier retrieved at Eastleigh. Customs had been most co-operative.

Roger Scaife turned the package gently in his hands. His palms were broad, his fingers slim and sensitive – in keeping with the restless expression, the thin bony frame and hair falling to his collar.

'We'll run the test immediately,' he said, 'I'll call you at six. Better still, where are you staying? I'll bring the results over.'

'That's really kind,' said Emma. 'I'm at the Hilton. But Roger, it's true isn't it, that this blood-test will make a great deal of difference?'

'Well, we certainly hope so. But you of all people should know the problems. Though our findings are most encouraging, no one can predict when this will become a routine test.'

'But eventually you expect to eliminate existing ambiguities?'

'Again – we hope so. Presently "adult death syndrome" is put on the death certificate at many post-mortems. But this means the doctors simply don't know what happened. They know there's been a weird heart arrhythmia, but haven't a clue what caused it. Now at least we'll be able to say.'

'So let me leave you to it,' said Emma, and thanked him again.

At a quarter past six the call came and she went down. As she went over to the reception she felt a twinge of anxiety. Half of her wanted her hunch to be right, since it would place another piece in the jigsaw. But half didn't, since it would increase her turmoil. He refused a drink, so she led the way over to a quiet corner. He handed over the printout and said 'It's completely clear cut. There is no doubt at all.'

'What does the test depend on?' asked Emma.

'Well we've discovered two enzymes that can be used as indicators for this particular cause of death. Most of our time has been spent in getting the sensitivity of the assays as sophisticated as possible. And, of course, I ran the test in conjunction with one for B.IgE antibody.'

'The immunoglobulin molecule on the surface membrane of the mast cells?' queried Emma.

'You keep up, I see. By the way, Emma, who's the patient? Do you want me to talk to his doctors or anything?'

'I didn't even tell you his gender,' smiled Emma. 'But yes, it was a man. But no, I'm in touch with his son and I'll tell him directly. Thanks Roger, I'm very grateful.'

She was glad he had not pressed her.

Next morning at Eastleigh Airport, Emma once more indulged – and once more loved every single moment. Yes, I could certainly get accustomed to this, she thought again. She had been met and steered smoothly through Customs and Immigration. At the bottom of the telescopic steps into the small jet she hesitated just a moment and smiled inwardly. Bring my sables and send for the photographers again. Then she ran lightly up the steps to be welcomed on board by a hostess, while the young man who had met her went up to the cockpit. But within two seconds he returned and said: 'Dr Austen, our Commandant wonders whether you would like to ride up front for take-off?'

Emma accepted with alacrity. Strapped in the jump-seat behind the pilot, she was fitted with headphones to monitor the conversations with the control tower and they taxied off. The plane soared up like a lark, straight into an ocean of clear blue sky. She heard the notes of the violin soaring too, against the soft counterpoint of Vaughan Williams' strings. Divine,divine – her soul seemed to take wings.

Once on course, the pilot took off his headphones and turned to her with a broad smile.

'Laurent Olivier at your service, Madame. Did you enjoy that?'

She smiled delightedly at the name and the strong young face. Black hair swept back straight over his head; trim moustache, olive complexion. Some Spanish blood, somewhere.

'My goodness, I did,' said Emma. 'But tell me something. As we were going down the runway I noticed there were none of the usual bumps. How come?'

He smiled charmingly. 'That was very observant, Madame. You gauged the essence of a good pilot, one who makes his passengers as comfortable as possible.'

'What do you mean?'

'Well, right down the centre of all runways is a line of lights. The nose-wheel hits these systematically and that's the accelerating bumps you feel in large planes. But any pilot worth his salt lines up the aircraft ever so slightly to the right, so his passengers don't feel a thing. And that's exactly what I did.'

'What's this plane?'

'*Le Mystère 20* – produced by Dassault. It's been so successful in America that it's been renamed "The Falcon" – international marketing reasons or some such. But we French pilots prefer *Mystère*. So I'll take you to Brussels. You knew Commissioner Marais, Madame?'

'I did some work with him.'

'A lovely gentleman. I flew him many times. But once he took up his post in the Commission he qualified for GLAM flights.'

'GLAM for glamorous?'

He laughed and waved his hand. 'No, Madame. *Groupe de Liaison Aérienne Interministérielle*. All government staff and top ranking officials in France fly with GLAM, but then you're taken to Villacoublay Airport, not Le Bourget.'

'This is such fun I don't care where you take me. Are you really Laurent Olivier – the famous...?'

'...Pilot! Indeed I am. You pay me a great compliment, Madame. So where shall we go?'

Emma had time to consider only a few glamorous alternatives while devouring coffee, croissants and a morning paper. Arriving at Zaventem – Brussels' international airport

– and still feeling like royalty but also something of an imposter, she thanked the crew, danced lightly down the steps and into Immigration and Customs. Her bag was carried outside, and there, by a waiting car, was Thierry.

She was delighted to see him. If she was going into battle once more, she wouldn't be alone. Once again, in the image of his father, he kissed her hand but then, unlike his father, kissed her gently on both cheeks. As her suitcase was placed in the boot, she watched him intently. She felt comfortable with him; she liked his quiet air of courteous authority – something of the aristocrat but little of the *énarque*; much of the pragmatic American, but much too, of the ancient French family. The combination could well prove irresistible.

Driving into Brussels he turned to look at her, serenely relaxed in the comfort of the car; the mushroom-coloured jacket easing over her shoulders, the blouse, lying not quite smoothly over the outline of her breasts.

'You've gone to an awful lot of trouble, Emma. I'm grateful.'

'Well, thank you for making this trip so easy.'

'And...?'

She didn't hesitate for a minute. 'I know how your father died. I don't know why or rather maybe the why is part of the how, or perhaps there's a completely separate why,' she continued, lamely.

He laughed – she was not usually this inarticulate – but looked relieved.

'Tell me later. I've arranged for lunch at home. I felt we would want to be alone.'

He waited until coffee was served and the maid had retreated.

'Now, tell me,' he invited, then suddenly changing his mind, got up from the chair and said, with eagerness in his voice, 'Let's take a walk. It's not such a bad day.'

The last time they had been in that room she had been breaking sad news. They were going to discuss this again and he wanted to be somewhere else.

In the hall he said, 'It will be chilly by the lake, so wear this,' and opened a closet, retrieved a large jacket, helped her in and wrapped a wool scarf around her neck.

'You look so much better now.'

At the end of the Square, they edged round fighting warriors and away to the right into Bois de la Cambre, then walked briskly downhill to a rough, gravel path above the lake. The setting was beautiful: the grass sloped down in steep banks towards the water; there was sunlight filtering through the leaves making dappled moving patterns on the ground.

They walked in silence. Emma was determined not to hurry him.

Then from below they heard the sound of a splash, a bark and laughter. The cry of *'tu es méchant'*, came up from the lake, quickly followed by a wet German Shepherd who proceeded to shake himself all over Emma. Following the dog up the muddy slope came a young man and a girl, both repeating *'méchant'* in voices totally devoid of anger. The girl held a plastic football which had been bitten to pieces; the boy was laughing; the dog wagged his tail in delight.

His mood well and truly broken, Thierry laughed, took Emma's hand, and led her to a green bench seat. On the back someone had sprayed 'Denis' and then an undecipherable squiggle.

'Who the hell was Denis?' said Thierry as he sat down, 'Never mind, I don't think I care. Now tell me.'

'Thierry, your father died from massive anaphylactic shock. The tests at Southampton proved this conclusively.'

'Why didn't Dewiere pick it up in the post-mortem?'

'Because the test is so new no one knows anything about it.'

'So how did you?'

'Well we're in the middle of a study for a pharmaceutical company about how long it takes for scientific results to get into general medical practice. We're following this test as one example.'

He took firmer hold on her hand. 'Please go on.'

'Now,' said Emma, 'I believe your father had acquired a rapid sensitivity to something – and I think I know what this was. By rapid, I mean it had set in over a short period of time. Even so, it's possible his death could have been a sheer accident for which no one is to blame. But on the other hand – and I'm trying to be a judicious mixture of lawyer, detective and scientist, as well as cover all my bases.'

'Emma, is this why you said that the "how" and the "why" of Papa's death might be one and the same thing, though then again they might not?'

'If it was not an accident, then the how and the why *become* the same thing. Who chose the lunch menu? I'd like to know. You and I believe something sinister was going on. Your father was investigating fraud in DG VI. He had suspicions, particularly about Fede. He wondered about that car coming at him. And Arthos...'

'...Oh yes, the young Musketeer...'

'...knows much more than he'd told me earlier. I forgot to mention: he's back in Paris right now. He called to say that Fede had given him his *congé*. He also said he wanted to see me, for he had learnt something the Commissioner would have wished to know. He was very insistent.'

'Does he have any suspicions about my father's death?'

'None at all – I'm quite sure about that. He was devastated but accepted the diagnosis without question.'

'But, Emma. You still haven't given me any details.'

'If I haven't it's because I still don't know them. I hope to know them when I've seen Arthos and the chef who prepared that lunch.'

'Perhaps we should both see them,' said Thierry.

'That's a good idea,' responded Emma. 'It's coming together fast, Thierry. I think we may be nearly there. By the way another weird thing also happened when I was at the Dorchester.'

'What was that?'

'I bumped into Céline Bardot coming out of the bar with Sir Robert Partridge.'

'Who he?'

Emma laughed. Thierry must have read the history of the *New Yorker*: for where else could he have picked up the classic query of Harold Ross, the magazine's most famous editor?

'Well, he's a lascivious man in Cambridge. A flaming Socialist and terribly rich too – no one quite knows how! But he knows more about the history of the Commission than anyone in England. Céline was completely flummoxed when she saw me and made some lame excuse about seeking advice about retirement.'

'Why would she retire? From what Papa told me, she was a pillar of the Directorate, and after a few more years, could draw a nice pension and probably end by being a consultant too.'

'That's exactly what I asked myself,' said Emma.

A wind had got up and the first mist appeared on the water. Emma became troubled by ghosts. Thierry saw her shiver, rose and said, 'Let's go home.' He put her arm through his as they made their way back, asked: 'Could Céline have had anything to do with the fraud?'

'I've wondered about that. She was as well-placed as anyone. She's been there forever; she must know her way into everybody's filing cabinet and computer program. She's probably got a master-key to all the doors, and having been in the *cabinet* so very long, people must believe she was tremendously influential.'

'So it would have been as easy as hell for her to trot along and say "the Commissioner wants this, so don't argue. Just give this contract to Edith Cresson's favourite dentist." '

'Thierry, you mustn't say that. She'll sue you.'

He grinned down at her: 'Just let her try. But have you any evidence that Céline was involved?'

'Only circumstantial. Actually, if I'm truthful, none at all. But she does make me suspicious.'

'What do you feel about Fede?'

'Well, just as well placed as Céline. Your father felt he had evidence, but that too, was circumstantial. There's a tendency to blame the Italians automatically because of association with the classic Mafia, and the fact that Italy's been heavily involved in many scams. But I know he's unscrupulous and he's also in cahoots with his own government.'

'Where could we get hard evidence?'

'God knows. Your father didn't have any and we certainly don't. Though I bet UCLAF does.'

'But I couldn't get anything out of them, nor could my father. Any better ideas?'

'None at all. We know the direct approach is not going to work, because we tried. So we'll have to take the indirect one and that means Arthos and the chef of the President's dining-room. Then – perhaps – we can fill in some details. But I've no idea how to get in to see the chef.'

'Oh, that's easily taken care of. Most appropriate for a son to offer reassurances to the man who cooked his father's last meal.'

CHAPTER EIGHTEEN

The Compliments of the Chef

*They may talk as they please about what they call pelf
and how pleasures of thought surpass eating and drinking.
My pleasure of thought is the pleasure of thinking
How pleasant it is to have money, heigh-ho!
How pleasant it is to have money.*

Arthur Hugh Clough: *Les Vaches*

Next morning they left early on the Thalys train to Paris. During the journey they spoke little, wrapped in their own thoughts, but praying this was the beginning of the end.

At Gare du Nord they took a taxi to the Ile St Louis, in the shadow of Notre-Dame. Though Thierry had an apartment on the island they had arranged to meet Arthos at the Jeu de Paume, a small hotel off a tiny side street. Centuries back the building had been first a barn, then an ancient tennis court. The walls surrounding the old court, climbed for three storeys. The ancient roof timbers were still exposed – criss-crossing, soaring, supporting – in a beautiful but functional, structural tangle.

Thierry led the way up the stairs to a quiet area at the back – a narrow space with one sofa, two armchairs and a table. Within ten minutes Arthos arrived and coffee was ordered.

He was subdued – obviously disconcerted to find the Commissioner's son with Emma. Thierry noticed this at once.

'Dr Austen tells me,' he began somewhat formally, 'that you have some information that might have interested my father.'

Now Arthos looked even more disconcerted. He gave Emma a glance which was almost pleading, but Thierry was not going to leave them and his voice had carried more than a touch of his father's authority.

'Yes,' he said, 'I needed to talk.'

Emma decided to lend a hand.

'Arthos, when I dropped in to see you, just before I left Brussels, I asked if you had found out anything about fraud within DG VI. You said no. Quite frankly, I didn't believe you. So what's on your mind now?'

Now he looked relieved.

'That was the second time I told you a lie. I did so because I was a coward, and because I was a coward, I made a mistake.'

'What do you mean?' asked Emma.

Thierry stayed silent, recognising that Arthos would talk more easily to Emma for his adoration was obvious. To his amused horror, he was aware of prickles of jealousy. Stop it, he told himself: he's years younger.

Emma sensing the sexual dynamics, was highly amused.

'Why did you want to see me?' she asked again, gently.

'I really needed to talk to someone outside the House,' said Arthos. 'I have made a terrible mistake – I know.' He sighed.

'Come,' Thierry's voice was now gentle.

Arthos turned to him.

'You will be aware, Dr Marais' he said, 'that your father was anxious to eliminate fraud within his Directorate. The Quatraro affair and the whole business of the

Parliamentarians censure on the Commission had made such an impact, that he decided to take a stand. He thought that the *chef*, Dr Felice Fede, was the source of the fraud.'

'Why Fede?' asked Thierry. 'Did he have any hard evidence?'

'None that I knew of, though I was told...'

'...by your Finnish girl friend in UCLAF...?' prompted Emma.

'Yes. However, she said that UCLAF were not yet revealing what they suspected to anyone and certainly not to the Commissioner.'

'Why not?' said Thierry again.

'The usual story. The internal rules are so protective of the Commission that UCLAF has to be very careful. Not everything is sweetness and light within the House. Some people hate each other, others are jealous, most are territorial. Others like Paul van Buitenen genuinely do suspect and blow the whistle only...'

'To be fired for their pains,' observed Emma.

'Paul van Buitenen...?' For one moment Thierry couldn't place him.

'...a middle-ranking – Grade B – Dutch Eurocrat,' Arthos had the information at his fingertips. 'He'd been in the Commission for eight years before he joined the Financial Control team in January 1998. He was so appalled at the frauds and the cover-ups and croneyism he was finding, that he sent a dossier to the Euro MPs, but only after trying the proper channels and being totally frustrated. The President said van Buitenen's action was deplorable and he was suspended. A whispering campaign began – saying he was mad!'

'I remember now,' said Thierry.

'The Commissioner was outraged at his treatment. And that's one reason why his investigations began. But there were other reasons, too. The Claude Perry business for a start.'

'Claude Perry?' asked Emma.

'A former Paris nightclub singer with lots of business interests, one of which was to provide temporary staff to the Commission. Van Buitenen handed over a dossier allegedly full of "convincing evidence" that over a hundred officials may have been "corrupted" by payments from Perry's companies.'

'All in cash?'

'Not at all – mobile telephones, holidays, computers, BMWs. These officials drew up fake employment contracts and then took a cut. There were heaps of incriminating documents. But there were other reasons to look at Fede.'

'Which were?' prompted Emma.

'Well, the Quatraro affair was in the background and the Italians always in the news. You've surely heard about the ghostly herd of subsidised cows that apparently lives in a Rome office block? Then there was a row with their dairy farmers. The rules said the Italian government should have fined them for overproduction of milk, but didn't. So the Community calculated the fines due and deducted the sum from the next lot of grants. The Italian government was incensed and there was a massive demonstration by furious farmers.

'A whole heap of other illegal practices were going on. I know that Commissioner Marais would never subscribe to the syllogism: "all members of the Mafia are Italian; he is an Italian, therefore he must be a member of the Mafia." But there were many genuine reasons to look in the direction of Fede. He's known to be not totally scrupulous, whenever it suits him.'

'Why did he move you on?' asked Emma.

'Well, he didn't find me with my hand in the till or my eyes devouring the files. But my style irritates him and he suspected – quite rightly – that I had an *entrée* to UCLAF that he didn't. And I was learning things that a *chef de cabinet* ought to know, but I wasn't about to tell him.'

'And he maintains close relationships with his government?'

'You noticed it at the meeting, did you? Reassuring his Minister about tobacco subsidies? Yes, he keeps in very close contact with his government but so too, does Willi Dashöfer. Still the Commissioner was completely on the wrong track.'

'Well, if my father was on the wrong track, then so were we.'

Arthos looked astonished.

'Yes, we know a great deal about all this.'

'May I ask how, Dr Marais?' Arthos was genuinely surprised.

'I would be happy to tell you. While I was going through my father's effects I came across a most comprehensive dossier he had assembled. He gave a clear indication who he suspected. But he couldn't get any information out of UCLAF at all. Since Dr Austen met me around that time and had obviously had a good working relationship with my father, I shared the dossier with her and together we tried to work out what was troubling him.'

Arthos looked at Emma with a mixture of adoration and respect.

'So that's why you came back into Breydel that day, and started...forgive me, Madame Austen...noseying around?'

'Yes, indeed,' admitted Emma. What's sauce for the goose is sauce for the gander, she reminded herself. Arthos had not been completely open with her, but neither had she with him.

'But what's troubling you is more than thinking Commissioner Marais was looking at the wrong person, isn't it?' she continued.

'Oh, yes. I knew who he ought to be looking at.'

Emma decided to take a chance. 'Céline Bardot?'

'Whatever made you think of her?'

'Several reasons. She was more perfectly placed than anyone else; she knew the workings of the Commission inside out; she was high enough up the hierarchy to influence people lower down.'

Before she continued she glanced at Thierry, who nodded agreement.

'She was always around with the files at very odd times and on two occasions I caught her not merely dissembling, but lying. This struck me as unusual, for she seemed so good – too much so to be true, actually. But if you looked at her detachedly, she provided the most perfect cover-up.'

'All that's so,' nodded Arthos. 'But do you know where she is now?'

'No. The last time I saw her was in the Dorchester Hotel in London.'

Arthos suddenly went very quiet. 'So you don't know where she is now?' he repeated.

Emma looked at him and her heart sank.

'No.'

'She's in hospital. She's had a complete breakdown. She's in a very bad way.'

'Why?'

'Don't you see?' he said impatiently. 'She was on to the fraud, not perpetrating it. Somehow, somewhere, papers fell into her hands. She knew the Commissioner was examining files and she was too. She became like a nervous ferret, digging the stuff out. But the more she found the more upset she became and completely went to pieces.'

'The pillars of her temple crashing down,' said Emma. 'Terribly sad.'

'Very sad,' Arthos repeated, 'But I knew who the Commissioner ought to be looking at.'

'How did you find out?' asked Emma.

'Because finally I did get access to some UCLAF files. I was able to read the papers which formed the case they were building against one *cabinet* member. Please don't ask me how I was given this access. I shall find it very embarrassing if I have to tell you.'

Emma gave a faint smile: oh, your beautiful blonde, she thought. Thierry stifled a grin.

'Why wouldn't UCLAF tell my father?'

'You've already asked me that. Since the Commissioner had made his zeal most publicly obvious I think they hoped he would find out for himself. But we were dancing around each other – the Quatraro affair all over again. We don't admit problems exist. The silence of the subsidies – I'm sure you've heard that phrase,' he said, turning to Emma.

'Many times.'

'Everything conspires to prevent the facts emerging. But UCLAF had another difficulty. It was the same one I had.'

He hesitated. Emma heard faint sounds from the reception desk below. Someone checking out.

'Which was?' she asked very gently.

'How could UCLAF challenge the Commissioner with the truth? But I could have. I should have; I was close to him but I just didn't know how to begin even. How could I say, "it's not your *chef* you should be investigating; it's your mistress".'

There was a stunned silence. Thierry looked as if he had been poleaxed. Emma felt pity for the young man but was too shattered to say so.

'I can't believe it. I can't believe it,' Thierry sounded angry.

'It's true. She was up to her neck.'

'Who blew the whistle on her?'

'Well, the Financial Controller picked up a number of discrepancies.'

'We knew this bit,' said Thierry, 'from my father's dossier.'

'Then a Danish woman came in on the national hot line. Generally these people give information anonymously. Though they're asked to leave a contact number, most prefer not to do so. But unusually she did. So someone from UCLAF made contact and was given full details. Sybilla's fingers were touching contracts, subsidies, transit fraud. She must have made a packet.'

Emma remembered the house on Avenue Fond'roy, furnished expensively, the dinner parties, the lavish lifestyle, the careless arrogance that comes with never having to think about money.

'Anyone behind her?'

'Who knows?'

'Was she working with anyone else in the Directorate?'

'We're not quite sure, though we know she'd a tame computer expert. I always meant to ask you, Madame Austen: were your files ever tampered with?'

'A number of times.'

'This doesn't surprise me.'

'Why would anyone believe an unknown source calling from Copenhagen?'

'Well, it turns out that she wasn't as unknown as all that. UCLAF did a little digging in Copenhagen and this person had been in prison for three years for allegedly being involved in drugs. They couldn't pin anything on her so eventually she was released. But she knew what she was talking about all right.'

'But why did she shop Sybilla?'

Again he replied: 'Who knows? There was a suggestion – ' and his face wrinkled in some distaste – 'that there was a strong sexual element.'

Thierry braced himself.

'Your father was one of her lovers, but she took many others and most were women.'

He was steamrollering Thierry and Emma into believing what he was saying.

Thierry expelled a breath in a deep rush and shook his head.

'I know,' said Arthos, 'I understand what you're feeling. I never liked her and now I hate her. Her deception was total. She liked to give the impression that she came from a wealthy aristocratic Danish family. Not a bit of it. Her father was a gambler and a rogue. He made and lost a couple of fortunes in rapid succession, then finally shot himself. Her sister now runs a crummy bar near the harbour in Copenhagen.'

'Oh no.' This was Emma.

'She became furious with the Commissioner eventually.'

'Why?' This was Thierry.

'Well, he refused to confirm her permanent appointment into the Commission. She was a *sousmarin*, and such people generate a lot of resentment for they're placed by Commissioners or Director-Generals who want their people where they can exert pressure and do favours. But Commissioner Marais totally refused. This wasn't personal – he wouldn't do it for anyone. I saw her in the office shortly after his pronouncement. She was livid for she badly wanted status and influence. And of course, the more influence she had the more she knew, and the more she knew the more she could make. So whether you believe it or not, that's where the Commissioner should have been looking.'

And us too, thought Emma, but it never even crossed our minds. Oh God, what a tangle.

'Arthos,' she said, 'who from the *cabinet* was responsible for that press release after the Commissioner died? Was it...'

'Yes, it was. You'll remember how quickly she agreed when you said it was urgent to have the hospital make a formal announcement. Shortly after you'd left, she told Dr Fede that he could safely leave the matter in her hands. But is this relevant?'

Again Emma looked at Thierry and again he nodded.

'No,' said Emma, untruthfully.

'Anyway, I'm deeply sorry. I'm sorry because the Commissioner is dead. I admired him and loved working with him. I'm sorry that I didn't face up to what I ought to have done no matter how difficult.' His face appeared to crumble.

Thierry rose and put his arm around the younger man's shoulder.

'There's no need to be sorry. But generally it's best to say what has to be said. You'd have learnt that from my father.'

'I learnt many things from your father.'

Thierry squeezed Arthos' shoulder.

'I don't want you to worry at all. It was a terrible dilemma; you did what you thought right.'

As the two men shook hands, Emma smiled and said, 'I'll walk you down.'

They went down the staircase, through the lobby and across the courtyard to the enormous old wooden doors that led to the street.

'Arthos,' she said, 'thank you so much for coming. I tell you: this has been very important. But where's your Finnish goddess now?'

'Do you know, Madame Austen, perhaps it's about time I found out.'

'That's an excellent idea. You do just that.'

And as he turned to leave, she moved forward and gently kissed him on both cheeks.

Back upstairs she found an exhausted Thierry slumped in the chair.

'My father could have been spared this,' he said.

'In a sense he was,' said Emma.

'Yes, thank God, but *quelle salade!*'

She'd never heard the phrase before but guessed he wasn't talking about lettuce. As she slipped down on the sofa by Thierry and he reached for her hand, she felt a surge of warmth, ready to relax in the enjoyment of their relationship. But the job was not yet finished.

Thierry spent much of the train journey back to Brussels wondering how plausible the chef would find his pretext. In the event Antoine Cronje, the Chief Chef of the President's Dining-Room, was most co-operative. The suggestion that Thierry was greatly distressed that such a tragic event should have occurred at Antoine's special lunch, was sufficient for him to invite Dr Marais to come in during the afternoon. At that time he was off duty.

If he was surprised that Thierry Marais arrived accompanied by an English lady, *très distinguée,* he gave no sign, but greeted her with exquisite politeness as companion to the Commissioner's son.

Antoine, known to be superb at his job, looked as though he never ate a thing for he was thin as a rake. Emma felt he could probably fit into his chef's hat. He spent far too long indoors, for he was sallow, with a precise and nervous air.

He pulled up two chairs, apologised for the cramped conditions in his office, which could just hold a desk, a bookcase and a telephone. Then he and Thierry exchanged mutual compliments about the various merits of Provençal cooking – Antoine's home territory – and those of the Auvergne. Finally he raised the subject that was on everyone's mind.

'What an appalling tragedy, Monsieur,' Antoine said. 'I was quite overcome.'

Emma could easily see him having an attack of the vapours.

'Your father was such a courteous gentleman, who always took trouble to thank everyone for their services. All of us feel the loss dreadfully, though none, of course, more deeply than you. I'm only so thankful that though the sad event occurred at a lunch which it was my privilege to create, clearly nothing was wrong there, for your father alone was ill.'

'*Bien sûr*,' said Thierry. 'I appreciate your concern and also your relief. Though my father's heart attack was unexpected, we have no doubt that eventually some simple medical reason – stress perhaps – will be found to be the cause. Your menu was exquisite, I understand.'

'Well, monsieur, who can resist demonstrating the riches of our Provençal cuisine? *Brandade* is a dish of great simplicity, but delicious as a first course.'

'I'm really interested in the ending of the meal,' said Emma. 'I understand there was an unusual dessert which contained a number of, shall we say, sinful ingredients.'

Antoine laughed, rose to his feet, and moved towards the shelves at the right of his desk.

'I would not call chocolate sinful, Madame,' he said, 'not if you use the best varieties such as *Valhona* – which is, naturally, French.'

He handed a book to Emma.

'There, Madame, on page one you will find everything you wish to know.'

The cover read *The Book of Chocolate* published by Flammarion of New York. On page one she saw an extract from another book, *Sweet Temptation* by Jeanne Bourin. Thierry leant over her shoulder and together they read:

Another memorable delight was béhanzin. *This fabulous cake, no doubt because of its high chocolate content, bore the name of the last King of the Dahomey, whose sad fate it was to be deported to Algeria after his Kingdom was conquered by our ancestors. That, however, is of no importance, and indeed when I was seven or eight years old, I didn't give a fig for these historical details, whereas the* béhanzin, *on the contrary, afforded me untold pleasure.*

It was a square cake made up of a series of alternate layers of the finest chocolate butter cream and a light hazelnut paste. Covered in chocolate powder, it had the dark velvety appearance of a beautiful dark chestnut, fully doing justice to is name.

'The Kingdom of Dahomey?' queried Emma.

'Present day Benin,' said Thierry. 'Between Ghana and Nigeria.'

'I know cocoa butter comes from Ghana, but not hazelnuts surely?'

'No, of course not,' replied Antoine, 'But, I have no difficulty for I obtain my hazelnut paste from Lenotre, who manufactures it in France. The base, however, is a pure nut praline guaranteed to come from Piedmont.'

Hearing the words 'Piedmont' and 'hazelnut paste', Emma recalled the Sainsbury's advertisement. The yoghurt was incorrectly labelled as 'low fat toffee' but was in fact 'hazelnut'. She felt the adrenalin surge: the final pieces of the jigsaw were now in place.

'It's extremely difficult to work, though the results can be wonderful.'

'Why so?' asked Thierry.

'The method depends on the ambient temperature, so you must change proportions according to whether it's winter or summer. In winter you must use a hundred grams of hazelnut paste for every kilo of cocoa butter and fifteen grams of recovered milk. But in summer you must use equal proportions.'

'There has to be a reason,' said Emma.

'It has to do with the oil content.' The chef seemed to strengthen as he spoke. 'Actually some chefs believe it's best to work the paste at body temperature, for you can test it with your lips. It must be neither hot nor cold.'

'But other than that, is the recipe straightforward?'

There was no way Antoine was going to admit that.

'Well, no; fine cooking is never easy. One has to be extremely careful and given the occasion, this was not a dish I would have permitted my subordinates to prepare. I made the cake myself. In fact I was so anxious that I did a trial run a few days before.'

Emma looked at Thierry, who returned her gaze. But Antoine had caught the exchange and a flicker of apprehension came over his face.

'Monsieur,' he enquired, 'there is, I trust, no suggestion that anything was wrong.'

'Absolutely none at all,' said Thierry reassuringly. 'I'm no cook, but what you say is most interesting.'

'And for me too,' interjected Emma, 'as a scientist, the intricacies of your procedures, dictated by the characteristics of the materials with which you brilliant chefs work, are as fascinating as any used by a chemist in a laboratory.'

She thought that was pretty good – horribly pompous and deeply flattering at one and the same time.

'I am reassured,' said Antoine. But he was not. 'I'm always most anxious to please,' he continued, then hesitated. 'And of course, in this particular instance, I was more than happy to follow the suggestion of one of your father's *cabinet* members, who actually recommended I offered this dessert and indeed, stood by my side while I did a trial run.'

Once again Thierry eyed Emma; once again Antoine caught the look.

'And that would be...?' Thierry finally prompted.

Now Antoine did not hesitate.

'Really, monsieur, there are only two cooks of genius in this town. And she is the other one. May I offer you a cognac?'

CHAPTER NINETEEN

Tea for Three

...Somewhere I would find a new life.
Nothing is ever as definite as that.
If you love a human or an animal there are great ropes pulling you back
to the object of that love, and the hands that haul upon the
ropes are you own.

Gavin Maxwell: *Raven Seek Thy Brother*

At half past two the following afternoon, Thierry and Emma were in the drawing-room of Marais' house, awaiting the final act. Emma had spent the entire morning wrestling with the props. They had an hour or so before the principal arrived.

'Now,' said Thierry, 'please – the details?'

'Thierry, as I said earlier, your father died from massive anaphylactic shock, a reaction to something he ate during that lunch. This is unlikely to have been the smoked cod and certainly not the British beef, but probably the hazelnuts in the dessert.'

'Sorry to interrupt, but are you saying that Papa had a fatal allergy to hazelnuts?'

'That's exactly what I'm saying.'

'But that's unbelievable. Frenchmen eat hazelnuts all the time. Certainly my father did. Or are you also saying it's possible suddenly to become fatally allergic to something you've tolerated before?'

'That too,' said Emma. 'There are many examples of delayed sensitivity. Wasp stings are one, strawberries another. Some people happily gorge every summer yet one year weals appear on their arms. When penicillin first came in doctors noticed that while some patients showed no reaction at all and some had an immediate one, others slowly acquired a sensitivity, through having too small doses over a long period of time.

'Allergy to nuts is now recognised as a very serious problem. But it's an odd one. Some children are born with a sensitivity to peanuts, so even infants can die suddenly. Others acquire it. In 1997 a British bio-chemist, visiting Idaho, didn't even eat them. He was twenty-eight and just touched a few, then happened to brush his hand across his mouth. Within minutes a terrible swelling occurred. He quickly washed out his mouth and took an anti-histamine pill. But though the ambulance came at once he died in the hospital. Then we have about 30,000 cases in the UK of allergy to sesame seeds, that generally does not develop until after the age of thirty. Hazelnuts are another case in point. About two hundred cases of suddenly acquired allergy have occurred.'

'And the blood-test in Southampton confirmed this in the case of my father?'

'Yes. Southampton was a lucky break. We've never had a blood-test before that can confirm death from anaphylactic shock. But my friend – Roger Scaife – and his group have developed tools that can detect the products released from mast cells.'

'What are mast cells?'

'Special cells of the immune system. In anaphylactic shock, they explode and release histamine and anti-inflammatory materials into the blood, including two enzymes, *tryptase* and *kinase*. These are the indicators of an allergic explosion. Of course, Roger would have liked to have had the stomach contents analysed, but it wasn't necessary. I knew it had to be hazelnuts.'

Suddenly Thierry stood up and smote his forehead.

'*Tiens*. That explains something. When Papa told me he was having an affair I was happy for him. I really was. He missed my mother so much and I was glad he had found some comfort. But he also confessed that it nearly didn't happen for it started on the wrong foot completely – though foot is perhaps not the appropriate word.

'He said that when Sybilla first asked him to dinner she offered him a liqueur – the hazelnut one they'd been offered in Piedmont. He remembered how sick he'd been on the mission, so refused. But she pressed him and he drank. Then suddenly his face went red and he felt awful and the whole evening ended in total humiliation. But go on.'

'Well, what do we really know for sure? One: we know your father died of a massive allergic reaction to hazelnuts; two, he may not have realized this, but it's likely Sybilla suspected, for those two quite separate episodes would have alerted her; three, we also know that she suggested this hazelnut dessert to Antoine.'

'But it's not a sure fire way of getting my father out of the way,' said Thierry.

'If her guess was right, it was. So natural it was completely foolproof. She merely gave a very firm shove to a process that had already begun.'

'What was her motive?'

'At first I couldn't think of anything other than money and power,' said Emma, 'But Arthos gave us another, of course.'

'She wanted to parachute into a permanent position but my father was stopping the practise.'

'Exactly.'

'Murder for such a minor reason?'

'Not minor at all. She stood to lose everything.'

'If all this is true, what can we do about it?'

'Well, that's the hell of it. I don't think we can do anything. Even a stupid lawyer could punch so many holes in this case that it would be as leaky as a colander.'

'You're right. I can just imagine LeQuesne's reaction when I trot in to him and say "I knew you were suspecting Sybilla Høgstrøm and, by the way, she murdered my father." But, Emma, having got this far, we must wrap it up. When she comes should we accuse her directly?'

'It's risky. We're not skilled at interviewing.'

The next hour was the longest Emma could remember. At first Thierry was restless but finally sat down. He looked awfully tired, noticed Emma. Suddenly he asked: 'Did you get to know her at all?'

'Not really,' replied Emma. 'She once took me to Bruges for a weekend. She had some business there, she said. It was delightful. I did a couple of touristy things – like the obligatory 30-minute boat ride from Dijver and climbed the Tower in the Markt. Then we went down to T'Zand and had a vast fish stew. I was thankful I'd had the exercise.'

'You would have certainly got it.'

'The view was worth every step. But I tried to dig a little – I was genuinely interested. Had she any brothers or sisters; had she travelled a lot? I didn't get very far. The answer was yes, to both the questions, but that was all.'

Thierry rose. 'Let's have some music. I need soothing.'

What would he choose? Poulenc – gentle, undemanding and calming.

As he sat back listening, she watched him and tried to sort out her own emotions. His face was finally in repose, its features now very familiar. Was it only two months ago since she had left Cambridge, confident that Brussels would not disturb her ordered serenity so deliberately structured? And here she was, trying to solve the murder of a man she had so admired while sitting opposite his son – the scion of an ancient, wealthy French family – by prior arrangement with the father.

Probably Marais' plan had been to arrange a series of meetings – drinks that first night; dinner, perhaps, when they returned from Italy; an invitation to visit in Paris and the family estate in Auvergne. There would have been time and space to test feelings and experience a new lifestyle in a country that was not her own.

What would have happened then; what consequences would have followed had Charles Marais' scenario unfolded to its very end? She would have had to uproot from Components and Cambridge. Could she do this? Possibly. Could she have continued with her work? Surely. These were modern times, not the constricted ones of Louis XIV.

But that scenario could never take place. She had been precipitated into a maelstrom of violence, danger and murder. Criminal activities and political machinations had sucked her down into a whirlpool, so suddenly and so shockingly that her emotions were still in a complete tangle. The sadness, the waste and the anger swirled around, but so too did the compassion, the sympathy and growing affection for Thierry. Unbelievable that the one single factor responsible for the whole tangle was the greedy actions of a member of the European Awkward Squad. *Quelle salade*, indeed.

Thierry watched Emma, deep in her reverie – the soft curl of hair falling to the collar, the smooth, pink complexion, the slight wrinkle of the nose when something distasteful had either been said or she suspected was about to be said, the cool, calm competence, the vitality and humour. Papa knew what he was about, he thought gratefully.

Emma was so lost in her own thoughts that when the bell rang she shot up, like a startled fawn.

Thierry laughed, got to his feet, put out his hands and pulled her up from the sofa.

'The last act,' he said, 'Whatever happens, I want you to know how grateful I am.'

'For what?'

'For setting up the end-game.'

Though Sybilla couldn't really figure out why Thierry Marais had invited her to tea, she was confident she could make him extremely happy that he had. She arrived on the dot of 4 p.m.

She had dressed beautifully, though quietly. She was full of condolences; she was discreetly flirtatious. He showed her the sitting-room and the study and the painting on the wall. On his father's desk he had randomly scattered some papers as if he had been working through the files, though he had removed those notes that indicated Marais' suspicion of Fede.

She admired the décor, made informed remarks about the Fra Angelico painting. Then back in the salon she went to the bay windows and observed: 'What a charming square – so quiet, so exclusive. Many distinguished people have lived here. The Lord Carrington was one, when he was Secretary-General of NATO.'

'But there are dark shadows in the woods beyond.'

Surprised, she turned and graced him with a dazzling smile.

'So morose, I do not like to think of such things.' She moved closer. 'Your father bought this house, I believe?'

'Yes and I'll be keeping it.'

'You are going to join us in Brussels? That would be delightful.'

'It's possible.'

'And you would not find it difficult to acquire a position of influence in this city. You are a man of many interests.'

'As you are a woman of many interests.'

'I should indeed hope so,' and stepped still closer.

Then the front door bell rang.

'Ah, the maid's off this afternoon. Excuse me while I answer the door. Please make yourself at home.'

Quickly he left the room. He had deliberately left open the folding doors to the study. He had guessed correctly. Sybilla strolled through and began reading the papers scattered on the desk. As she was reading a jingle came into her mind and she began humming.

'Me no worry, me no care, me go marry a millionaire... If he die...'

Hearing footsteps she returned to the drawing-room and stationed herself under one of the family portraits, looking at it with what she hoped was a skilled gaze. But behind her Thierry was silent – so fixing a dazzling smile upon her face she turned round...and saw Emma, who had just placed a tea tray on the table.

She tried not to look as deflated as she felt.

'Emma, I didn't know you were in Brussels.'

Emma gently adjusted her scarf and with deliberate ambiguity, said 'Well, there were a number of investigations I had to complete. These are intriguing times in the College.'

Sybilla had no idea what Emma was talking about, so resorted to a lame 'Yes, they are.'

'And how is everyone else?' asked Emma. '...Céline?...'

Her question was interrupted as Thierry, looking remarkably cheerful, came in with the sugar bowl and placed it on the tray.

'How do you like your tea?' he asked Sybilla.

'Weak, with lemon, please.'

As he poured, he looked at Emma with an air of intimacy 'You like it weak too, I know, but with just a little milk.'

Sybilla took the cup and sat down. Assessing the new situation, she gave a mental shrug as the second line of the jingle came into her head.

'*If he die, me no cry, me go marry other guy.*'

'You were asking about Céline. It's terribly sad. She's in hospital.'

'Oh no! What's wrong?' asked Emma.

'A breakdown. But there: she was totally obsessive about the College.'

'And I suppose those delightful young Musketeers have returned to Paris,' Emma ventured. 'You will miss those three merry men?'

'Not all of them. Arthos was quite unsuitable.'

'Not an *énarque*, you mean?' This was Thierry.

'True, not an *énarque*, but also too brash. I've often wondered about his background.'

'But Dr Fede. I trust he's well?'

Sybilla now looked so cheerful that Emma made a guess.

'He's invaluable I hope he has managed to establish you permanently in the House.'

Sybilla put down her tea cup, and shook her head, but only in response to Thierry's 'May I pour you another cup?'

How did Emma know so much? Well, it didn't matter.

'Yes. My appointment to the permanent staff is assured. Dr Fede was very glad to do this for me.'

I bet he was, murmured Emma to herself. What did you offer in exchange?

'Well, that's as may be, but perhaps Dr Fede should glance over his shoulder from time to time.' Thierry had intervened again. 'For who knows, the next Commissioner may be just as scrupulous as my father.'

'I don't quite understand.' She was looking so innocent.

200

'Well, fallout from the recent scandals is still around. My father had compiled a dossier. He had uncovered a major source of fraud in DG VI – his *cabinet* was a good place to hide.'

Sybilla lent forward and retrieved a small napkin from the table, then delicately wiped her lips.

'I am deeply surprised. To know that such venality existed at the very heart of Commissioner Marais' *cabinet*. Surely not his *chef*... Dr Fede...'

'Oh, but it wasn't Fede,' interjected Emma, 'nor Céline, poor soul. She was only close to identifying who it was. But Arthos knew and his information is totally reliable.'

Sybilla dabbed her lips again. 'You continue to surprise me.'

'Oh, I don't think so at all,' said Thierry, 'I don't think so at all.'

'Emma, you seem to have learnt a great deal during your time with us.'

Emma laughed cheerfully.

'I should hope so.'

Thierry got up, took Emma's cup and poured more tea, then turned to Sybilla. 'When my father died I understand you were responsible for arranging the hospital bulletin. Most thoughtful of you.'

'Did I? I really can't remember. The shock was too great, and...' The unspoken words hung in the air... 'I was your father's lover and understandably deeply distressed.'

'Well, it really doesn't matter who was responsible. But as it turns out the diagnosis was totally wrong. I wasn't satisfied with the hospital's findings, so I asked Dr Austen to help me establish just what happened.'

'That was wise. Given the circumstances, it is always better to know the truth.'

'So we are finding. Emma,' and he turned to her, 'perhaps you would tell Sybilla what turned up. You see,' he said to

Sybilla, 'Dr Austen suggested that blood samples be sent away for a special test, and this proved...'

Emma took up the refrain.

'...that Commissioner Marais died of anaphylactic shock.'

'Such difficult medical terms. I'm afraid I've no idea what that is.'

'Actually, it's not at all difficult,' said Emma, as briskly as if she were giving a lecture. 'It's massive immunological breakdown. The whole immune system goes into an explosive shock which can be fatal unless treatment is given immediately.'

'You see, Sybilla,' she went on very sweetly, 'until recently, doctors faced with a death – where there was no reason to suspect immunological problems – had no alternative but to put this down to heart failure.'

There was a long silence. They were both watching Sybilla intently but she gave no reaction.

'So the Commissioner was suffering from a disease of his immune system?'

'No, not at all,' murmured Thierry. 'Not a disease. It was enough that he had a fatal allergy.'

'To something in the air – like pollen?'

'To something in the food – at the lunch.'

'The food? How most unfortunate. What a tragic accident.'

Now Thierry's voice was angry.

'Tragic it certainly was, but it was no accident. This was deliberate.' He hesitated. 'Someone knew my father had this problem and planned the menu to provoke his death.'

'Dr Marais, you are insane.'

Thierry made no comment, but turned to Emma. 'Darling Emma, I'm awfully hungry. Didn't you bring a cake for tea?'

Emma giggled inwardly at his mischievous use of the endearment.

'Well, yes I did. How stupid of me to have forgotten. I'll fetch it.'

Back within two minutes, she placed the plate down on the table, looked directly at Sybilla and said 'With the compliments of the *chef*. I made it this morning, under Antoine's personal guidance. It's very difficult to work the hazelnut paste, but I had no problem, and neither did he – because you had stood by him when he did a trial run.'

'What are you talking about?' asked Sybilla.

Thierry took up the litany.

'You tell us. We know you suggested to Antoine that he serve *béhanzin* at the lunch.'

'And, so...?'

'You knew my father's weaknesses and you caused his death.'

'You forget yourself. I will listen no longer.'

'You will listen much longer.'

Sybilla rose.

'To think I believed you were truly your father's son. But you are just a stupid, hysterical young man.'

Now Thierry was on his feet.

'You were with him in Piedmont when he became ill. Later, the first night you expected to become his lover, you gave him the same liqueur. You saw he was acutely sensitive and you guessed the next exposure might be fatal. So you arranged to kill him.'

'I'm leaving.'

He barred the way.

'Dr Marais, remember your manners!'

'Not quite yet. We haven't finished. How could you...'

By now Emma was up, white and shaking, but she took up the refrain.

'The hospital's mistake was highly convenient. You thought no one could ever tell. Six months ago that would have been true. But I took the blood sample myself to the only place in the world that does the test. They confirmed why the Commissioner died at lunch.'

Emma spoke, could she see the colour drain away from Sybilla's face? Damn – not at all – utter wishful thinking. Now Thierry took over.

'Your motive – not a *crime passionel*. Oh no, you are far too selfish for that. But my father had learnt too much. He had built up an incriminating dossier and, as we now know, so too, has UCLAF.'

'Circumstantial raving,' said Sybilla, confidently, 'will convince no one.'

'I'm prepared to risk that. So much so that I've already written to the new President and the Belgian Police and the Danish Ambassador and my Ambassador and UCLAF and *European Voice* enclosing my father's dossier and our own conclusions. You're up to your neck in fraud. You conducted your corrupt activities well hidden, protected by the safety of your position in the *cabinet,* your affair with my father and the procedures whereby the Commission continues to protect its own.

'But like Quatraro before you, the time comes when the game is finally up. Public disgrace will be the least, prison the likeliest.'

Everyone stood as still as the birds in the tapestry – formal, symbolic, dead. Then Sybilla shook her head and turned a venomous look upon the one person who had started all this nonsense.

'Who would have imagined the Awkward Squad could be so awkward?' she said lightly.

Emma was blisteringly angry and her face showed it. 'I would. Oh, yes, I would.'

Did she detect a trace of fear? Not one little bit – not even unease. For with her usual regal omniscience, Sybilla Høgstrøm swept from the room.

Like children playing Grandmother's Footsteps, they stood until the slam of the front door released them. Emma was still white. Thierry bent down to the tray.

'Tea for two, I think...or, something stronger?' in an echo of their first meeting.

Emma shook her head, sat down and took the cup.

'Have you really made those copies and sent them around?'

'No. It was total bluff. I didn't have time and anyway my father's dossier would not have been useful. He suspected Fede.'

'But she wasn't to know?'

'Emma, I made a complete mess of it.'

'Why do you say that?'

'Because if I had been clever I could have got her to admit something.'

'I very much doubt it. She's the kind of person that would protest total innocence even if she were caught with a dead body on the floor, a smoking gun in one hand and pulling money out of the safe with the other. She's convinced she's invincible.'

'Yet I know she killed him. But, Emma, what's the use?' Now he really was distressed. 'She's right of course. UCLAF may have tight evidence, but *won't* do anything. Ours is all circumstantial and we *can't* do anything. Even if we could get Commission officials to take this murder seriously – which they wouldn't – and even if the police believed we had enough evidence to arrest her – which we don't – do you seriously expect that any court of law would convict?'

'No, quite honestly, I don't.'

'Nor do I. Not a chance. My father...,' and suddenly he slammed a fist hard into his other palm and cried out: 'So where's the beef?' and broke down.

She left him to weep only briefly, then moved behind his chair, held her arms close to his chest and placed her head by his. For a few minutes they rested together. Then gently he released himself, rose, pulled her towards him and kissed her hungrily.

She responded instantly to his embrace – aroused and loving. She liked this man – the son of his father – so much. Yet as she did so one small part of her mind thought: if this were a steamy novel, we'd be tearing our clothes off and in bed in two minutes flat.

But it's not like that – not just yet. There was still too much pain and, she knew, too much uncertainty on her part. Was she ready for such a profound change in life. Relinquish Cambridge, take risks again. Did he sense this?

Perhaps he had for slowly he released her. 'Emma,' he said, 'I love you – really love you. But...?'

'Dearest Thierry.'

'Too much is happening, too fast. When I make love to you I want it to be as carefree and as joyous as possible.'

'And so do I. So what now?'

'Dearest Emma. Next week we're having a gathering at our home in the Auvergne – a chance for my father's friends to say a final goodbye. Would you come?'

'Of course I'll come.'

'Then afterwards, we'll spend an enormous amount of time together.'

'Let's.'

Sybilla Høgstrøm calmly hailed a taxi in the Chaussée de Waterloo. Once back at the Avenue Fond'roy, she went immediately to the telephone and dialled a number. In a small village, some ten kilometers west of Waterloo, the phone was allowed to ring twice. Then with slow deliberation, the Spider picked up the receiver, but said nothing.

She could not contain her anxiety.

'They know.'

'Who knowth?'

'His son. That English woman. They have files; they are sending them around to everyone.'

'Unlike you to be so thupid. I'm thurprithed. They're bluffing.'

'But...'

'Pull yourthelf together.' His voice could be so cold.

'I succeeded where you failed.' That was a mistake. One never mentioned 'failure'.

There was silence. What a stupid woman, he thought. All we did was to warn him.

'You have no reathon to worry. We'll take care of you. Haven't we alwayth?'

She had to admit this was true – the house, the lavish lifestyle, the influence, the glamour. And those divine bank deposits that underpinned them all – in Switzerland and Luxembourg. What a useful little country the smallest in the European Union was proving to be, with its secret banking and spurious foundations that could shelter tax, launder funds and hide loot. She would do her damndest to see that Denmark never voted for tax harmonisation.

But she'd had to work so very hard for all this. True, her first job – the merest favour – suggested during a small reception at the Commission, had been so easy to engineer. But as the years had gone by, other suggestions had been made of increasing importance. Soon she had been sucked down into a thrilling and rewarding way of life, only to have everything she had struggled for placed in jeopardy through an administrative decision by a stubborn peasant from the Auvergne. Still, it was all over now: she was safe.

But he was still speaking.

'Tho thtay calm. Have a drink or bake a cake.'

She shuddered and hung up.

CHAPTER TWENTY

Across the River

"Shepherd, yonder across the river, surely you are not having much fun?"
Sing bailero, lero, etc.
"None at all, and are you?"...
"Shepherd, the river runs between us, and I cannot get across!"
"Then I will come and fetch you."

Bailero: *Chants d'Auvergne*, Canteloube

Emma chose to drive down to the Auvergne. She needed the space and the time that the changing landscapes of France would provide. Driving the old Napoleonic roads through France was one of her special joys. She once had taken a magnificent run from the Pyrenees right through to Dieppe – some seven hundred and fifty miles of almost empty roads – passing through small towns only and meeting just a few lorries the entire way.

She took two days for the journey and arrived refreshed. The setting was incomparable. Off the motorway that ran south from Clermont-Ferrand, a small road ran east, parallel with a line of trees that once formed a long avenue heading from the château towards the mountains.

Neither just a service nor a concert, the occasion of Marais' remembrance was simple and wonderfully appropriate. Guests assembled in the Orangerie across from the château's main entrance. Only a few words of remembrance were spoken – from people who worked on the estate and who had known Marais for years and from Thierry and his sister, Josephine. Above all there was music – heart-rending and consoling. Some she didn't know; some – Verdi and Fauré she did.

When it had finished she moved with the other guests across the gravel courtyard and through the tall doors into the main salon. The east facing windows and tall French doors were open; the weather softly tranquil. She walked out on to the terrace and caught her breath.

She had emerged from a quintessential eighteenth-century French château, into an English park landscape that could have been laid out by Capability Brown. From the gravel terrace, running the entire length of the house and punctuated by some twenty-five orange trees set in decorative antique pots, the sloping lawn ran down to a large S-shaped lake. A single black swan sadly sailed passed; three white ducks paddled frenetically.

But her eyes were drawn way across the park and fields to a small town in the distance, set on a cone-shaped hill, one of *Les Clefs* – the Keys – of the Auvergne. The spine of the region, a mountain chain that runs north to south, was once an area of fearsome volcanoes. But all around are 'pepper pots' of hills that millions of years ago had puffed out their larval contribution, too. Everything was exquisite – just exactly as it was. What on earth, Emma thought, did the family of Giscard d'Estaing think it was doing, ruining it all by a Volcano Theme Park? The exquisite reality was enough.

As she turned to go back indoors someone stopped her.

'Excuse me, Madame. You are Dr Austen?'

'Yes.'

'I'm sorry to trouble you but there is a call from your office in Cambridge. They say it's urgent. Would you follow me please?'

Emma was led through a series of rooms furnished with family portraits, heirlooms and antiques, to a small red study. She picked up the phone.

'Emma,' There was something in Jane's voice – anxious, relieved, tearful. 'Thank God, you're alive! Are you really all right?'

'Of course I'm all right. What on earth's the matter?'

'Emma. Emma,' Jane repeated. 'Sit down and listen carefully. Something's happened.'

Emma had to listen for a full five minutes. She was shocked but said only. 'Thanks Jane. I understand. Of course, I'll go,' and replaced the receiver.

Slowly she made her way back into the salon and stood gazing out across the park. Then she turned to look across the room and saw him, politely and courteously, working his way through the guests. His sister, Josephine – a gentle woman with a tranquil face – was with him. Suddenly he lifted his head and caught Emma's eyes. He excused himself, walked over, took both her hands and kissed her.

'How good of you to come.'

'I found it most moving. Thierry, what a wonderful place this is.'

'I knew you'd like it.' He turned her back towards the windows. 'The park was designed by a pupil of Capability Brown. We imported him specially from England – at great expense, no doubt.'

He put his arm over her shoulder and they stood side by side for a while in silence. The single black swan swam around, aimless and depressed.

'We had a pair, but six months ago a fox killed the female.'

Emma reached up with her right hand until she found his.

'He's terribly lonely. He needs company so much that sometimes he makes his way to the swimming pool and gets in with us all. We have a devil of a time getting him back to the lake.'

'Shall you get another one?'

'We ought to – if we can keep the predators at bay. But Emma, we must all let our pasts go.'

She knew he was right, but there was no way they could – just yet and she had to tell him. But wanting to preserve the peace of their shared moment, she prevaricated yet again.

'Did you hear, Thierry? UCLAF's finished. There's a new fraud prevention office – OLAF. It's supposed to have total independence and more powers. There's even talk of criminal investigations against some of Santer's Commissioners.'

Thierry exploded: *'Bon Dieu, il était plus que temps!'*

'What did you say?'

'I'm sorry. That was very vulgar. You British might have said "high bloody time!".'

'And there's more. The auditors have found a litany of abuses and sharp practices in the European Parliament too – which, of course, the Parliamentarians fiercely deny. What I find unbelievable is everyone's indignation when these are pointed out. Too righteous for words. They act like they think it's a game – as if all that peculation was standard procedure.'

'But it was, wasn't it? Corrupt from the start. If Mitterand really was bribing Kohl so as to get the political decisions he wanted, then no wonder that ethos pervaded the whole Commission and no one was shocked. But I am – to the core – and I'm not convinced matters will change. The new outfit will go on turning up high levels of fraud, while the Commission will just hope the problem will go away. But it won't: the level of external criminal involvement is too large.'

He calmed down. 'You're staying tonight, of course.'

'I'm afraid I've got to leave at once.'

His face clouded. 'Emma, impossible. Why?'

'Thierry, Jane has just called from Cambridge.'

'And?'

'A detective from Scotland Yard turned up in our offices along with a French gendarme from Marquise. I gather it's a small village not far from Calais. They were asking questions about me.'

Thierry looked at her, horrified. 'Why?'

Again Emma hesitated, then took a deep breath. 'A woman was washed up on the shore near Wissant. They showed photographs of the body to Jane and from the description they gave, I suspect it was Sybilla.'

'Dear God in heaven. Do they know how she got there?'

'They've no idea at all.'

Suicide? Shades of Quattraro, thought Emma, unhappily.

'Retribution? But whose, Emma?'

'God knows.'

'Anyway, this then is the end.'

'I'm afraid it may not be.'

'Emma, dearest, what do you mean?'

'The only thing on the body was my business card. That's why they went to Cambridge. And that's why Jane wondered if I was dead. Anyway, I'm told I must report to the Gendarmerie in Boulogne.'

He knew she had to go. They'd come looking for her if she didn't. In fact, he'd bet even money that tomorrow morning, an inspector from Clermont-Ferrand would be pounding on the château gates.

'Jane told them that you were here?'

'Oh, yes. I don't think she had any alternative.'

'Of course she didn't. I'll come with you.'

'No. No. You've too much to do here. I'll be all right.'

He smiled, but looked anxious.

'Clearly, I have to come to terms with thoroughly independent Emma. I'll follow up tomorrow. Do you have a mobile phone? Call me.'

'Yes, I've got one.'

He tightened his arm around her shoulders, 'I don't want to lose you too, Emma. Come back soon. We open the château in the summer for all our friends. Promise you'll come back then?'

She had no difficulty with that.

'Of course, I'll come back.'

'Then go safely. Please, please take care.'

And he kissed her.

She was in no hurry to face the fresh, disruptive reality so she chose to drive back over the mountains. In any case she wanted to make private farewells to Charles Marais in his own landscape. As the road climbed through the uplands towards the sky, she could see the gathering clouds piling higher and higher, darkening to grey, then jet black. A storm was brewing. Something calm would see her through, so she pressed the radio button for *France Musique*, expecting an illustrated talk about an obscure fourteenth-century lutenist, or some such.

She had to pull off the road very quickly, for she was crying uncontrollably. Canteloube's poignant notes flooded the car, the voice of the girl calling to the shepherd across the water.

She got out, walked over to a wall, leant on the stones and looked west. She was in deep countryside, yet in the field behind the stone wall there was a simple granite cross. She couldn't make out why, for there was no writing on the stone, no graveyard nearby. But where the arms of the cross intersected they were touched by a rainbow as the rays of the setting sun refracted through the advancing storm. God rest his soul.

She watched transfixed and allowed her tears to run their course. She knew that they were the final mourning for the father. But she still did not know how deep yet was her love for the son.

HOUSE OF STRATUS

Internet: www.houseofstratus.com including author interviews, reviews, features.

Email: sales@houseofstratus.com please quote author, title and credit card details.

Hotline: UK ONLY: **0800 169 1780**, please quote author, title and credit card details.

INTERNATIONAL: **+44 (0) 20 7494 6400**, please quote author, title and credit card details.

Send to: **House of Stratus Sales Department**
24c Old Burlington Street
London
W1X 1RL
UK